THE MIDDLEMAN

AND OTHER STORIES

BHARATI MUKHERJEE

PENGUIN BOOKS

Penguin Books India (P) Ltd., 210 Chiranjiv Towers, 43 Nehru Place. New Delhi-110019, India
Penguin Books Ltd., 27 Wrights Lane, London W8 5TZ, UK
Penguin Books USA Inc., 375 Hudson Street, New York, N.Y. 10014, USA
Penguin Books Australia Ltd., Ringwood, Victoria, Australia
Penguin Books Canada Ltd., 10 Alcorn Avenue, Suite 300, Toronto, Ontario M4V 3B2, Canada.
Penguin Books (NZ) Ltd., 182-190 Wairau Road, Auckland 10, New Zealand.

First published in the United States by Grove Press, New York 1988
First published in the U.K. by Virago Press Ltd. 1989
Published by Penguin Books India Ltd. 1990

Copyright © Bharati Mukherjee, 1988

10   9   8   7   6   5   4   3

Stories in this book first appeared in *Playboy, Mother Jones, Chelsea, The Literary Review;* and have been reprinted in *Best Canadian Stories, Best American Stories* of 1987, and *Editor's Choice,* 1987.
This work was completed under a grant from the National Endowment for the Arts.

For Clark

CONTENTS

THE
MIDDLEMAN

THERE are only two seasons in this country, the dusty and the wet. I already know the dusty and I'll get to know the wet. I've seen worse. I've seen Baghdad, Bombay, Queens—and now this moldering spread deep in Mayan country. Aztecs, Toltecs, mestizos, even some bashful whites with German accents. All that and a lot of Texans. I'll learn the ropes.

Forget the extradition order, I'm not a sinful man. I've listened to bad advice. I've placed my faith in dubious associates. My first American wife said, in the dog-eat-dog, Alfred, you're a beagle. My name is Alfie Judah, of the once-illustrious Smyrna, Aleppo, Baghdad—and now Flushing, Queens—Judahs.

I intend to make it back.

This place is owned by one Clovis T. Ransome. He reached here from Waco with fifteen million in petty cash hours ahead of a posse from the SEC. That doesn't buy much down here, a few thousand acres, residency papers and the right to swim with the sharks a few feet off the bottom. Me? I make a living from things that fall. The big fat belly of Clovis T. Ransome bobs above me like whale shit at high tide.

The president's name is Gutiérrez. Like everyone else he has enemies, right and left. He's on retainer from men like Ransome, from the *contras*, maybe from the Sandinistas as well.

The woman's name is Maria. She came with the ranch, or with the protection, no one knows.

President Gutiérrez's country has definite possibilities. All day I sit by the lime green swimming pool, sun-screened so I won't turn black, going through my routine of isometrics while Ransome's *indios* hack away the virgin forests. Their hate is intoxicating. They hate gringos—from which my darkness exempts me—even more than Gutiérrez. They hate in order to keep up their intensity. I hear a litany of presidents' names, Hollywood names, Detroit names—Carter, *chop*, Reagan, *slash*, Buick, *thump*—bounce off the vines as machetes clear the jungle greenness. We spoke a form of Spanish in my old Baghdad home. I always understand more than I let on.

In this season the air's so dry it could scratch your lungs. Bright-feathered birds screech, snakeskins glitter, as the jungle peels away. Iguanas the size of wallabies leap from behind macheted bushes. The pool is greener than the ocean waves, cloudy with chemicals that Ransome has trucked over the mountains. When toads fall in, the water blisters their skin. I've heard their cries.

Possibilities, oh, yes.

I must confess my weakness. It's women.

In the old Baghdad when I was young, we had the hots for blonds. We'd stroll up to the diplomatic enclaves just to look at women. Solly Nathan, cross-eyed Itzie, Naim, and me. Pinkish flesh could turn our blood to boiling lust. British matrons with freckled calves, painted toenails through thin-strapped sandals, the onset of varicose, the brassiness of prewar bleach jobs—all of that could thrill us like cleavage. We were twelve and already visiting whores during those hot Levantine lunch hours when our French masters intoned the rules of food, rest, and good digestion. We'd roll up our fried flat bread smeared with spicy potatoes, pool our change, and bargain with the daughters of washerwomen while our lips and fingers still glistened with succulent grease. But the only girls cheap enough for boys our age with unspecified urgencies were swamp Arabs from Basra and black girls from Baluchistan, the broken toys discarded by our older brothers.

Thank God those European women couldn't see us. It's comforting at times just to be a native, invisible to our masters. *They* were worthy of our lust. Local girls were for amusement only, a dark place to spend some time, like a video arcade.

"You chose a real bad time to come, Al," he says. He may have been born on the wrong side of Waco, but he's spent his adult life in tropical paradises playing God. "The rains'll be here soon, a day or two at most." He makes a whooping noise and drinks Jack Daniels from a flask.

"My options were limited." A modest provident fund I'd been maintaining for New Jersey judges was discovered. My fresh new citizenship is always in jeopardy. My dealings can't stand too much investigation.

"Bud and I can keep you from getting bored."

Bud Wilkins should be over in his pickup anytime now. Meanwhile, Ransome rubs Cutter over his face and neck. They're supposed to go deep-sea fishing today, though it looks to me as if he's dressed for the jungle. A wetted-down hand towel is tucked firmly under the back of his baseball cap. He's a Braves man. Bud ships him cassettes of all the Braves games. There are aspects of American life I came too late for and will never understand. It isn't love of the game, he told me last week. It's love of Ted Turner, the man.

His teams. His stations. His America's cup, his yachts, his network.

If he could clone himself after anyone in the world, he'd choose Ted Turner. Then he leaned close and told me his wife, Maria—once the mistress of Gutiérrez himself, as if I could miss her charms, or underestimate their price in a seller's market—told him she'd put out all night if he looked like Ted Turner. "Christ, Al, here I've got this setup and I gotta beg her for it!" There *are* things I can relate to, and a man in such agony is one of them. That was last week, and he was drunk and I was new on the scene. Now he snorts more JD and lets out a whoop.

"Wanna come fishing? Won't cost you extra, Al."

"Thanks, no," I say. "Too hot."

The only thing I like about Clovis Ransome is that he doesn't snicker when I, an Arab to some, an Indian to others, complain of the heat. Even dry heat I despise.

"Suit yourself," he says.

Why do I suspect he wants me along as a witness? I don't want any part of their schemes. Bud Wilkins got here first. He's entrenched, doing little things for many people, building up a fleet of trucks, of planes, of buses. Like Ari Onassis, he started small. That's the legitimate side. The rest of it is no secret. A man with cash and private planes can clear a fortune in Latin America. The story is Bud was exposed as a CIA agent, forced into public life and made to go semipublic with his arms deals and transfer fees.

"I don't mind you staying back, you know. She wants Bud."

Maria.

I didn't notice Maria for the first days of my visit. She was *here*, but in the background. And she was dark, native, and I have my prejudices. But what can I say—is there deeper pleasure, a darker thrill than prejudice squarely faced, suppressed, fought against, and then slowly, secretively surrendered to?

Now I think a single word: adultery.

On cue, Maria floats toward us out of the green shadows. She's been swimming in the ocean, her hair is wet, her big-boned, dark-skinned body is streaked with sand. The talk is Maria was an aristocrat, a near-Miss World whom Ransome partially bought and partially seduced away from Gutiérrez, so he's never sure if the president owes him one, or wants to kill him. With her thick dark hair and smooth dark skin, she has to be mostly Indian. In her pink Lycra bikini she arouses new passion. Who wants pale, thin, pink flesh, who wants limp, curly blond hair, when you can have lustrous browns, purple-blacks?

Adultery and dark-eyed young women are forever entwined in my memory. It is a memory, even now, that fills me with chills and terror and terrible, terrible desire. When I was a child, one of our servants took me to his village. He wanted me to see something special from the old Iraqi culture. Otherwise, he feared, my lenient Jewish upbringing would later betray me. A young woman, possibly adulterous but certainly bold and brave and beautiful enough to excite rumors of promiscuity, was stoned to death that day. What I remember now is the breathlessness of waiting as the husband encircled her, as she struggled against the rope, as the stake barely swayed to her writhing. I remember the dull thwock and the servant's strong fingers shaking my shoulders as the first stone struck.

I realize I am one of the very few Americans who knows the sound of rocks cutting through flesh and striking bone. One of the few to count the costs of adultery.

Maria drops her beach towel on the patio floor, close to my deck chair, and straightens the towel's edge with her toes. She has to have been a dancer before becoming Ransome's bride and before Gutierrez plucked her out of convent school to become his mistress. Only ballerinas have such blunted, misshapen toes. But she knows, to the right eyes, even her toes are desirable.

"I want to hear about New York, Alfred." She lets herself fall like a dancer on the bright red towel. Her husband is helping Eduardo, the houseboy, load the jeep with the day's gear, and it's him she seems to be talking to. "My husband won't let me visit the States. He absolutely won't."

"She's putting you on, Al," Ransome shouts. He's just carried a case of beer out to the jeep. "She prefers St. Moritz."

"You ski?"

I can feel the heat rising from her, or from the towel. I can imagine as the water beads on her shoulders how cool her flesh will be for just a few more minutes.

"Do I look as though I ski?"

I don't want to get involved in domestic squabbles. The *indios* watch us. A solemn teenager hefts his machete. We are to have an uncomplicated view of the ocean from the citadel of this patio.

"My husband is referring to the fact that I met John Travolta in St. Moritz," she says, defiantly.

"Sweets," says Ransome. The way he says it, it's a threat.

"He has a body of one long muscle, like an eel," she says.

Ransome is closer now, "Make sure Eduardo doesn't forget the crates," he says.

"Okay, okay," she shouts back. "Excuse me." and I watch her corkscrew to her feet. I'm so close I can hear her ligaments pop.

Soon after, Bud Wilkins roars into the cleared patch that serves as the main parking lot. He backs his pickup so hard against a shade tree that a bird wheels up from its perch. Bud lines it up with an imaginary pistol and curls his finger twice in its direction. I'm not saying he has no feeling for wildlife. He's in boots and camouflage pants, but his hair, what there is of it, is blow-dried.

He stalks my chair. "We could use you, buddy." He uncaps a beer bottle with, what else, his teeth. "You've seen some hot spots."

"He doesn't want to fish." Ransome is drinking beer, too. "We wouldn't want to leave Maria unprotected." He waits for a retort, but Bud's too much the gentleman. Ransome stares at me and winks, but he's angry. It could get ugly, wherever they're going.

They drink more beer. Finally Eduardo comes out with a crate. He carries it bowlegged, in mincing little half-running steps. The fishing tackle, of course. The crate is dumped into Bud's pickup. He comes out with a second and third, equally heavy, and drops them all in Bud's truck. I can guess what I'm watching. Low-grade arms transfer, rifles, ammo and maybe medicine.

"*Ciao, amigo*," says Bud in his heavy-duty Texas accent.
He and Ransome roar into the jungle in Ransome's jeep.

"I hope you're not too hungry, Alfie." It's Maria calling from the kitchen. Alfred to Alfie before the jeep can have made it off the property.

"I'm not a big eater." What I mean to say is I'm adaptable. What I'm hoping is, let us not waste time with food.

"Eduardo!" The houseboy, probably herniated by now, comes to her for instructions. "We just want a salad and fruit. But make it fast, I have to run into San Vincente today." That's the nearest market town. I've been there, it's not much.

She stands at the front door about to join me on the patio when Eduardo rushes us, broom in hand. "*Vaya!*" he screams.

But she is calm. "It must be behind the stove, stupid," she tells the servant. "It can't have made it out this far without us seeing it."

Eduardo wields his broom like a night stick and retreats into the kitchen. We follow. I can't see it. I can only hear desperate clawing and scraping on the tiles behind the stove.

Maria stomps the floor to scare it out. The houseboy shoves the broom handle in the dark space. I think first, being a child of the overheated deserts, giant scorpions. But there are two fugitives, not one, a pair of ocean crabs. The crabs, their shiny purple backs dotted with yellow, try to get by us to the beach where they can hear the waves.

How do mating ocean crabs scuttle their way into Clovis T. Ransome's kitchen? I feel for them.

The broom comes down, thwack, thwack, and bashes the shells in loud, succulent cracks. *Ransome, Gringo*, I hear.

He sticks his dagger into the burlap sacks of green chemicals. He rips, he cuts.

"Eduardo, it's all right. Everything's fine." She sounds stern, authoritative, the years in the presidential palace have served her well. She moves toward him, stops just short of taking his arm.

He spits out, "He kills everything." At least, that's the drift.

The language of Cervantes does not stretch around the world without a few skips in transmission. Eduardo's litany includes crabs, the chemicals, the sulfurous pool, the dead birds and snakes and lizards.

"You have my promise," Maria says. "It's going to work out. Now I want you to go to your room, I want you to rest."

We hustle him into his room but he doesn't seem to notice his surroundings. His body has gone slack. I hear the word Santa Simona, a new saint for me. I maneuver him to the cot and keep him pinned down while Maria checks out a rusty medicine cabinet.

He looks up at me, "You drive *Doña* Maria where she goes?"

"If she wants me to, sure."

"Eduardo, go to sleep. I'm giving you something to help." She has water and a blue pill ready.

While she hovers over him, I check out his room. It's automatic with me. There are crates under the bed. There's a table covered with oilcloth. The oilcloth is cracked and grimy. A chair by the table is a catchall for clothes, shorts, even a bowl of fruit. Guavas. Eduardo could have snuck in caviar, imported cheeses, Godiva candies, but it's guavas he's chosen to stash for siesta hour hunger pains. The walls are hung with icons of saints. Posters of stars I'd never have heard of if I hadn't been forced to drop out. Baby-faced men and women. The women are sensual in an old-fashioned, Latin way, with red curvy lips, big breasts and tiny waists. Like Maria. Quite a few are unconvincing blondes, in that brassy Latin way. The men have greater range. Some are young versions of Fernando Lamas, some are in fatigues and boots, striking Robin Hood poses. The handsomest is dressed as a guerrilla with all the right accessories: beret, black boots, bandolier. Maybe he'd played Che Guevara in some B-budget Argentine melodrama.

"What's in the crates?" I ask Maria.

" I respect people's privacy," she says. "Even a servant's." She pushes me roughly toward the door. "So should you."

* * *

The daylight seems too bright on the patio. The bashed shells are on the tiles. Ants have already discovered the flattened meat of ocean crabs, the blistered bodies of clumsy toads.

Maria tells me to set the table. Every day we use a lace cloth, heavy silverware, roses in a vase. Every day we drink champagne. Some mornings the Ransomes start on the champagne with breakfast. Bud owns an air-taxi service and flies in cases of Épernay, caviar, any damned thing his friends desire.

She comes out with a tray. Two plates, two fluted glasses, chèvre cheese on a bit of glossy banana leaf, water biscuits. "I'm afraid this will have to do. Anyway, you said you weren't hungry."

I spread a biscuit and hand it to her.

"If you feel all right, I was hoping you'd drive me to San Vincente." She gestures at Bud Wilkin's pickup truck. "I don't like to drive that thing."

"What if I didn't want to?"

"You won't. Say no to me, I mean. I'm a terrific judge of character." She shrugs, and her breasts are slower than her shoulders in coming down.

"The keys are on the kitchen counter. Do you mind if I use your w.c. instead of going back upstairs? Don't worry, I don't have horrible communicable diseases." She laughs.

This may be intimacy. "How could I mind? It's your house."

"Alfie, don't pretend innocence. It's Ransome's house. This isn't *my* house."

I get the key to Bud's pickup and wait for her by the bruised tree. I don't want to know the contents of the crates, though the stencilling says "fruits" and doubtless the top layer preserves the fiction. How easily I've been recruited, when a bystander is all I wanted to be. The Indians put down their machetes and make signs to me: *Hi, mom, we're Number One*. They must have been watching Ransome's tapes. They're all wearing Braves caps.

The road to San Vincente is rough. Deep ruts have been cut into the surface by army trucks. Whole convoys must have passed this way during the last rainy season. I don't want to know whose trucks, I don't want to know why.

Forty minutes into the trip Maria says, "When you get to the T, take a left. I have to stop off near here to run an errand." It's a strange word for the middle of a jungle.

"Don't let it take you too long," I say. " We want to be back before hubby gets home." I'm feeling jaunty. She touches me when she talks.

"So Clovis scares you." Her hand finds its way to my shoulder.

"Shouldn't he?"

I make the left. I make it sharper than I intended. Bud Wilkins's pickup sputters up a dusty rise. A pond appears and around it shacks with vegetable gardens.

"Where are we?"

"In Santa Simona," Maria says. "I was born here, can you imagine?"

This isn't a village, it's a camp for guerrillas. I see some women here, and kids, roosters, dogs. What Santa Simona is is a rest stop for families on the run. I deny simple parallels. Ransome's ranch is just a ranch.

"You could park by the pond."

I step on the brake and glide to the rutted edge of the pond. Whole convoys must have parked here during the rainy season. The ruts hint at secrets. Now in the dry season what might be a lake has shrunk into a muddy pit. Ducks float on green scum.

Young men in khaki begin to close in on Bud's truck.

Maria motions me to get out. "I bet you could use a drink." We make our way up to the shacks. The way her bottom bounces inside those cutoffs could drive a man crazy. I don't turn back but I can hear the unloading of the truck.

So: Bud Wilkins's little shipment has been hijacked, and I'm the culprit. Some job for a middleman.

"*This* is my house, Alfie."

I should be upset. Maria's turned me into a chauffeur. You bet I could use a drink.

We pass by the first shack. There's a garage in the back where there would be the usual large, cement laundry tub. Three men come at me, twirling tire irons the way night sticks are fondled by Manhattan cops. "I'm with her."

Maria laughs at me. "It's not you they want."

And I wonder, *who* was she supposed to deliver? Bud, perhaps, if Clovis hadn't taken him out? Or Clovis himself?

We pass the second shack, and a third. Then a tall guerrilla in full battle dress floats out of nowhere and blocks our path. Maria shrieks and throws herself on him and he holds her face in his hands, and in no time they're swaying and moaning like connubial visitors at a prison farm. She has her back to me. His big hands cup and squeeze her halter top. I've seen him somewhere. Eduardo's poster.

"Hey," I try. When that doesn't work, I start to cough.

"Sorry," Maria swings around still in his arms. "This is Al Judah. He's staying at the ranch."

The soldier is called Andreas something. He looks me over. "Yudah?" he asks Maria, frowning.

She shrugs. "You want to make something of it?"

He says something rapidly, locally, that I can't make out. She translates, "He says you need a drink," which I don't believe.

We go inside the command shack. It's a one-room affair, very clean, but dark and cluttered. I'm not sure I should sit on the narrow cot; it seems to be a catchall for the domestic details of revolution—sleeping bags, maps and charts, an empty canteen, two pairs of secondhand army boots. I need a comfortable place to deal with my traumas. There is a sofa of sorts, actually a car seat pushed tight against a wall and stabilized with bits of lumber. There are bullet holes through the fabric, and rusty stains that can only be blood. I reject the sofa. There are no tables, no chairs, no posters, no wall decorations of any kind, unless you count a crucifix. Above the cot, a sad, dark, plaster crucified Jesus recalls His time in the desert.

"Beer?" Maria doesn't wait for an answer. She walks behind a curtain and pulls a six-pack of Heinekens from a noisy refrigerator. I believe I am being offered one of Bud Wilkins's unwitting contributions to the guerrilla effort. I should know it's best not to ask how Dutch beer and refrigerators and '57 two-tone Plymouths with fins and chrome make their way to nowhere jungle clearings. Because of guys like me, in better times, that's how. There's just demand and supply running the universe.

"Take your time, Alfie." Maria is beaming so hard at me it's unreal. "We'll be back soon. You'll be cool and rested in here."

Andreas manages a contemptuous wave, then holding hands, he and Maria vault over the railing of the back porch and disappear.

She's given me beer, plenty of beer, but no church key. I look around the room. Ransome or Bud would have used his teeth. From His perch, Jesus stares at me out of huge, sad, Levantine eyes. In this alien jungle, we're fellow Arabs. You should see what's happened to the old stomping grounds, compadre.

I test my teeth against a moist, corrugated bottle cap. It's no good. I whack the bottle cap with the heel of my hand against the metal edge of the cot. It foams and hisses. The second time it opens. New World skill. Somewhere in the back of the shack, a parakeet begins to squawk. It's a sad, ugly sound. I go out to the back porch to give myself something to do, maybe snoop. By the communal laundry tub there's a cage and inside the cage a mean, molting bird. A kid of ten or twelve teases the bird with bits of lettuce. Its beak snaps open for the greens and scrapes the rusty sides of the bar. The kid looks defective, dull-eyed, thin but flabby.

"Gringo," he calls out to me. "Gringo, gum."

I check my pockets. No Dentyne, no Tums, just the plastic cover for spent traveller's checks. My life has changed. I don't have to worry about bad breath or gas pains turning off clients.

"Gringo, Chiclets."

The voice is husky.

I turn my palms outward. "Sorry, you're out of luck."

The kid leaps on me with moronic fury. I want to throw him down, toss him in the scummy vat of soaking clothes, but he's probably some sort of sacred mascot. "How about this pen?" It's a forty-nine cent disposable, the perfect thing for poking a bird. I go back inside.

I am sitting in the HQ of the Guerrilla Insurgency, drinking Heineken, nursing my indignation. A one-armed man opens the door. "Maria?" he calls. "*Prego.*" Which translates, indirectly, as "The truck is unloaded and the guns are ready and should I kill this guy?" I direct him to find Andreas.

She wakes me, maybe an hour later. I sleep as I rarely have, arm across my eyes like a bedouin, on top of the mounds of boots and gear. She has worked her fingers around my buttons and pulls my hair, my nipples. I can't tell the degree of mockery, what spillover of passion she might still be feeling. Andreas and the idiot boy stand framed in the bleaching light of the door, the boy's huge head pushing the bandolier askew. Father and son, it suddenly dawns. Andreas holds the birdcage.

"They've finished," she explains. "Let's go."

Andreas lets us pass, smirking, I think, and follows us down the rutted trail to Bud's truck. He puts the bird cage in the driver's seat, and in case I miss it, points at the bird, then at me, and laughs. Very funny, I think. His boy finds it hilarious. I will *not* be mocked like this. The bird is so ill-fed, so cramped and tortured and clumsy it flutters wildly, losing more feathers merely to keep its perch.

"*Viva la revolución, eh*? A leetle gift for helping the people."

No, I think, a leetle sign to Clovis Ransome and all the pretenders to Maria's bed that we're just a bunch of scrawny blackbirds and he doesn't care who knows it. I have no feeling for revolution, only for outfitting the participants.

"Why?" I beg on the way back. The road is dark. "You hate your husband, so get a divorce. Why blow up the country?"

Maria smiles. "Clovis has nothing to do with this." She shifts her sandals on the bird cage. The bird is dizzy, flat on its back. Some of them die, just like that.

"Run off with Andreas, then."

"We were going to be married," she says. "Then Gutiérrez

came to my school one day and took me away. I was fourteen and he was minister of education. Then Clovis took me away from him. Maybe you should take me away from Clovis. I like you, and you'd like it, too, wouldn't you?"

"Don't be crazy. Try Bud Wilkins."

"Bud Wilkins is, you say, dog meat." She smiles.

"Oh, sure," I say.

I concentrate on the road. I'm no hero, I calculate margins. I could not calculate the cost of a night with Maria, a month with Maria, though for the first time in my life it was a cost I might have borne.

Her voice is matter-of-fact. "Clovis wanted a cut of Bud's action. But Bud refused and that got Clovis mad. Clovis even offered money, but Bud said no way. Clovis pushed me on him, so he took but he still didn't budge. So—"

"You're serious, aren't you? Oh, God."

"Of course I am serious. Now Clovis can fly in his own champagne and baseball games."

She has unbuttoned more of the halter and I feel pressure on my chest, in my mouth, against my slacks, that I have never felt.

All the lights are on in the villa when I lurch Bud's pickup into the parking lot. We can see Clovis T. Ransome, very drunk, slack-postured, trying out wicker chairs on the porch. Maria is carrying the bird cage.

He's settled on the love seat. No preliminaries, no questions. He squints at the cage. "Buying presents for Maria already, Al?" He tries to laugh.

"What's that supposed to mean?" She swings the cage in giant arcs, like a bucket of water.

"Where's Bud?" I ask.

"They jumped him, old buddy. Gang of guerrillas not more'n half a mile down the road. Pumped twenty bullets in him. These are fierce little people, Al. I don't know how I got away." He's watching us for effect.

I suspect it helps when they're in your pay, I think, and you give them Ted Turner caps.

"Al, grab yourself a glass if you want some Scotch. Me, I'm stinking drunk already."

He's noticed Bud's truck now. The emptiness of Bud's truck.

"That's a crazy thing to do," Maria says. "I warned you." She sets the cage down on the patio table. "Bud's no good to anyone, dead or alive. You said it yourself, he's dog meat." She slips onto the love seat beside her husband. I watch her. I can't take my eyes off her. She snakes her strong, long torso until her lips touch the cage's rusted metal. "Kiss me," she coos. "Kiss me, kiss, kiss, sweetheart."

Ransome's eyes are on her, too. "Sweets, who gave you that filthy crow?"

Maria says, "Kiss me, loverboy."

"Sweetie, I asked you who gave you that filthy crow."

I back off to the kitchen. I could use a shot of Scotch. I can feel the damp, Bombay grittiness of the air. The rains will be here, maybe tonight.

When I get back, Ransome is snoring on the love seat. Maria is standing over him, and the bird cage is on his lap. Its door is open and Clovis's fat hand is half inside. The bird pecks, it's raised blood, but Clovis is out for the night.

"Why is it," she asks, "that I don't feel pride when men kill for me?"

But she does, deep down. She wants to believe that Clovis, mad jealous Clovis, has killed for her. I just hate to think of Maria's pretty face when Clovis wakes up and remembers the munitions are gone. It's all a family plot in countries like this; revolutions fought for a schoolgirl in white with blunted toes. I, too, would kill for her.

"Kill it, Alfie, please," she says. "I can't stand it. See, Clovis tried but his hand was too fat."

"I'll free it," I say.

"Don't be a fool—that boy broke its wings. Let it out, and the crabs will kill it."

Around eleven that night I have to carry Ransome up the stairs to the spare bedroom. He's a heavy man. I don't bother with the niceties of getting him out of his blue jeans and into his pajamas. The secrets of Clovis T. Ransome, whatever they are, are safe with me. I abandon him on top of the bedspread in his dusty cowboy boots. Maria won't want him tonight. She's already told me so.

But she isn't waiting for me on the patio. Maybe that's just as well. Tonight love will be hard to handle. The dirty glasses, the booze and soda bottles, the styrofoam-lidded bowl we used for ice cubes are still on the wicker-and-glass coffee table. Eduardo doesn't seem to be around. I bring the glasses into the kitchen. He must have disappeared hours ago. I've never seen the kitchen in this bad a mess. He's not in the villa. His door has swung open, but I can't hear the noises of sleeping servants in the tropics. So, Eduardo has vanished. I accept this as data. I dare not shout for Maria. If it's ever to be, it must be tonight. Tomorrow, I can tell, this cozy little hacienda will come to grief.

Someone should go from room to room and turn out the lights. But not me. I make it fast back to my room.

"You must shut doors quickly behind you in the tropics. Otherwise bugs get in."

Casually, she is unbuttoning her top, untying the bottom tabs. The cutoffs have to be tugged off, around her hips. There is a rush of passion I have never known, and my fingers tremble as I tug at my belt. She is in my giant bed, propped up, and her breasts keep the sheet from falling.

"Alfie, close the door."

Her long thighs press and squeeze. She tries to hold me, to contain me, and it is a moment I would die to prolong. In a frenzy, I conjugate crabs with toads and the squawking bird, and I hear the low moans of turtles on the beach. It is a moment I fear too much, a woman I fear too much, and I yield. I begin again, immediately, this time concentrating on blankness, on burnt-out objects whirling in space, and she pushes against me murmuring, "No," and pulls away.

Later, she says, "You don't understand hate, Alfie. You don't understand what hate can do." She tells stories; I moan to mount her again. "No," she says, and the stories pour out. Not just the beatings; the humiliations. Loaning her out, dangling her on a leash like a cheetah, then the beatings for what he suspects. It's the power game, I try to tell her. That's how power is played.

Sometime around three, I wake to a scooter's thin roar. She has not been asleep. The rainy season must have started an hour or two before. It's like steam out there. I kneel on the pillows to look out the small bedroom windows. The parking lot is a mudslide. Uprooted shrubs, snakes, crabs, turtles are washed down to the shore.

Maria, object of my wildest ecstacy, lies inches from me. She doesn't ask what I see. The scooter's lights weave in the rain.

"Andreas," she says. "It's working out."

But it isn't Andreas who forces the door to my room. It is a tall, thin Indian with a calamitous face. The scooter's engine has been shut off, and rain slaps the patio in waves.

"*Americano*." The Indian spits out the word. "Gringo."

Maria calmly ties her halter tabs, slowly buttons up. She says something rapidly and the Indian steps outside while she finds her cutoffs.

"Quickly," she says, and I reach for my pants. It's already cold.

When the Indian returns, I hear her say "Jew" and "Israel." He seems to lose interest. "*Americano*?" he asks again. "Gringo?"

Two more Indians invade my room. Maria runs out to the hall and I follow to the stairs. I point upwards and try out my Spanish. "Gringo is sleeping, drunk."

The revolution has convened outside Clovis's bedroom. Eduardo is there, Andreas, more Indians in Ted Turner caps, the one-armed man from Santa Simona. Andreas opens the door.

"Gringo," he calls softly. "Wake up."

I am surprised, truly astonished, at the recuperative powers of Clovis T. Ransome. Not only does he wake, but he sits, boots on the floor, ignoring the intrusion. His Spanish, the first time I've heard him use it, is excellent, even respectful.

"I believe, sir, you have me at a disadvantage," he says. He scans the intruders, his eyes settling on me. "Button your fly, man," he says to me. He stares at Maria, up and down, his jaw working. He says, "Well, sweets? What now?"

Andreas holds a pistol against his thigh.

"Take her," Ransome says, "You want her? You got her. You want money, you got that too. Dollars, marks, Swiss francs. Just take her—and him—" he says, pointing to me, "—out of here."

"I will take your dollars, of course."

"Eduardo—" Ransome jerks his head in the direction, perhaps, of a safe. The servant seems to know where it is.

"And I will take her, of course."

"Good riddance."

"But not him. He can rot."

Eduardo and three Indians lug out a metal trunk. They throw away the pillows and start stuffing pillow cases with bundles of dollars, more pure currency than I've ever seen. They stuff the rest inside their shirts. What must it feel like? I wonder.

"Well, señor Andreas, you've got the money and the woman. Now what's it to be—a little torture? A little fun with me before the sun comes up? Or what about him—I bet you'd have more fun with him. I don't scream, señor Andreas, I warn you now. You can kill me but you can't break me."

I hear the safety clicking off. So does Clovis.

I know I would scream. I know I am no hero. I know none of this is worth suffering for, let alone dying for.

Andreas looks at Maria as though to say, "you decide." She

holds out her hand, and Andreas slips the pistol in it. This seems to amuse Clovis Ransome. He stands, presenting an enormous target. "Sweetie—" he starts, and she blasts away and when I open my eyes he is across the bed, sprawled in the far corner of the room.

She stands at the foot of their bed, limp and amused, like a woman disappointed in love. Smoke rises from the gun barrel, her breath condenses in little clouds, and there is a halo of condensation around her hair, her neck, her arms.

When she turns, I feel it could be any of us next. Andreas holds out his hand but she doesn't return the gun. She lines me up, low, genital-level, like Bud Wilkins with a bird, then sweeps around to Andreas, and smiles.

She has made love to me three times tonight. With Andreas today, doubtless more. Never has a truth been burned so deeply in me, what I owe my life to, how simple the rules of survival are. She passes the gun to Andreas who holsters it, and they leave.

In the next few days when I run out of food, I will walk down the muddy road to San Vincente, to the German bar with the pay phone: I'll wear Clovis's Braves cap and I'll salute the Indians. "Turtle eggs," I'll say. "Number One," they'll answer back. Bud's truck has been commandeered. Along with Clovis's finer cars. Someone in the capital will be happy to know about Santa Simona, about Bud, Clovis. There must be something worth trading in the troubles I have seen.

_A_
WIFE'S
STORY

IMRE says forget it, but I'm going to write David Mamet. So Patels are hard to sell real estate to. You buy them a beer, whisper Glengarry Glen Ross, and they smell swamp instead of sun and surf. They work hard, eat cheap, live ten to a room, stash their savings under futons in Queens, and before you know it they own half of Hoboken. You say, where's the sweet gullibility that made this nation great?

Polish jokes, Patel jokes: that's not why I want to write Mamet.

Seen their women?

Everybody laughs. Imre laughs. The dozing fat man with the Barnes & Noble sack between his legs, the woman next to him, the usher, everybody. The theater isn't so dark that they can't see me. In my red silk sari I'm conspicuous. Plump, gold paisleys sparkle on my chest.

The actor is just warming up. *Seen their women?* He plays a salesman, he's had a bad day and now he's in a Chinese restaurant trying to loosen up. His face is pink. His wool-blend slacks are creased at the crotch. We bought our tickets at half-price, we're sitting in the front row, but at the edge, and we see things we shouldn't be seeing. At least I do, or think I do. Spittle, actors goosing each other, little winks, streaks of makeup.

Maybe they're improvising dialogue too. Maybe Mamet's provided them with insult kits, Thursdays for Chinese, Wednesdays for Hispanics, today for Indians. Maybe they get together before curtain time, see an Indian woman settling in the front row off to the side, and say to each other: "Hey, forget Friday. Let's get *her* today. See if she cries. See if she walks out." Maybe, like the salesmen they play, they have a little bet on.

Maybe I shouldn't feel betrayed.

Their women, he goes again. *They look like they've just been fucked by a dead cat.*

The fat man hoots so hard he nudges my elbow off our shared armrest.

"Imre. I'm going home." But Imre's hunched so far forward he doesn't hear. English isn't his best language. A refugee from Budapest, he has to listen hard. "I didn't pay eighteen dollars to be insulted."

I don't hate Mamet. It's the tyranny of the American dream that scares me. First, you don't exist. Then you're invisible. Then you're funny. Then you're disgusting. Insult, my American friends will tell me, is a kind of acceptance. No instant dignity here. A play like this, back home, would cause riots. Communal, racist, and antisocial. The actors wouldn't make it off stage. This play, and all these awful feelings, would be safely locked up.

I long, at times, for clear-cut answers. Offer me instant dignity, today, and I'll take it.

"What?" Imre moves toward me without taking his eyes off the actor. "Come again?"

Tears come. I want to stand, scream, make an awful scene. I long for ugly, nasty rage.

The actor is ranting, flinging spittle. *Give me a chance. I'm not finished, I can get back on the board. I tell that asshole, give me a real lead. And what does that asshole give me? Patels. Nothing but Patels.*

This time Imre works an arm around my shoulders. "Panna, what is Patel? Why are you taking it all so personally?"

I shrink from his touch, but I don't walk out. Expensive girls' schools in Lausanne and Bombay have trained me to behave well. My manners are exquisite, my feelings are delicate, my gestures refined, my moods undetectable. They have seen me through riots, uprootings, separation, my son's death.

"I'm not taking it personally."

The fat man looks at us. The woman looks too, and shushes.

I stare back at the two of them. Then I stare, mean and cool, at the man's elbow. Under the bright blue polyester Hawaiian shirt sleeve, the elbow looks soft and runny. "Excuse me," I say. My voice has the effortless meanness of well-bred displaced Third World women, though my rhetoric has been learned elsewhere. "You're exploiting my space."

Startled, the man snatches his arm away from me. He cradles it against his breast. By the time he's ready with comebacks, I've turned my back on him. I've probably ruined the first act for him. I know I've ruined it for Imre.

It's not my fault; it's the *situation*. Old colonies wear down. Patels—the new pioneers—have to be suspicious. Idi Amin's lesson is permanent. AT&T wires move good advice from continent to continent. Keep all assets liquid. Get into 7-11s, get out of condos and motels. I know how both sides feel, that's the trouble. The Patel sniffing out scams, the sad salesmen on the stage: postcolonialism has made me their referee. It's hate I long for; simple, brutish, partisan hate.

After the show Imre and I make our way toward Broadway. Sometimes he holds my hand; it doesn't mean anything more than that crazies and drunks are crouched in doorways. Imre's been here over two years, but he's stayed very old-world, very courtly, openly protective of women. I met him in a seminar on special ed. last semester. His wife is a nurse somewhere in the Hungarian countryside. There are two sons, and miles of petitions for their emigration. My husband manages a mill two hundred miles north of Bombay. There are no children.

"You make things tough on yourself," Imre says. He assumed Patel was a Jewish name or maybe Hispanic; everything makes equal sense to him. He found the play tasteless, he worried about the effect of vulgar language on my sensitive ears. "You have to let go a bit." And as though to show me how to let go, he breaks away from me, bounds ahead with his head ducked tight, then dances on amazingly jerky legs. He's a Magyar, he often tells me, and deep down, he's an Asian too. I catch glimpses of it, knife-blade Attila cheekbones, despite the blondish hair. In his faded jeans and leather jacket, he's a rock video star. I watch MTV for hours in the apartment when Charity's working the evening shift at Macy's. I listen to WPLJ on Charity's earphones. Why should I be ashamed? Television in India is so uplifting.

Imre stops as suddenly as he'd started. People walk around us. The summer sidewalk is full of theatergoers in seersucker suits; Imre's year-round jacket is out of place. European. Cops in twos and threes huddle, lightly tap their thighs with night sticks and smile at me with benevolence. I want to wink at them, get us all in trouble, tell them the crazy dancing man is from the Warsaw Pact. I'm too shy to break into dance on Broadway. So I hug Imre instead.

The hug takes him by surprise. He wants me to let go, but he doesn't really expect me to let go. He staggers, though I weigh no more than 104 pounds, and with him, I pitch forward slightly. Then he catches me, and we walk arm in arm to the bus stop. My husband would never dance or hug a woman on Broadway. Nor would my brothers. They aren't stuffy people, but they went to Anglican boarding schools and they have a well-developed sense of what's silly.

"Imre." I squeeze his big, rough hand. "I'm sorry I ruined the evening for you."

"You did nothing of the kind." He sounds tired. "Let's not wait for the bus. Let's splurge and take a cab instead."

Imre always has unexpected funds. The Network, he calls it, Class of '56.

In the back of the cab, without even trying, I feel light, almost free. Memories of Indian destitutes mix with the hordes of New York street people, and they float free, like astronauts, inside my head. I've made it. I'm making something of my life. I've left home, my husband, to get a Ph.D. in special ed. I have a multiple-entry visa and a small scholarship for two years. After that, we'll see. My mother was beaten by her mother-in-law, my grandmother, when she'd registered for French lessons at the Alliance Française. My grandmother, the eldest daughter of a rich zamindar, was illiterate.

Imre and the cabdriver talk away in Russian. I keep my eyes closed. That way I can feel the floaters better. I'll write Mamet tonight. I feel strong, reckless. Maybe I'll write Steven Spielberg too; tell him that Indians don't eat monkey brains.

We've made it. Patels must have made it. Mamet, Spielberg: they're not condescending to us. Maybe they're a little bit afraid.

Charity Chin, my roommate, is sitting on the floor drinking Chablis out of a plastic wineglass. She is five foot six, three inches taller than me, but weighs a kilo and a half less than I do. She is a "hands" model. Orientals are supposed to have a monopoly in the hands-modelling business, she says. She had her eyes fixed eight or nine months ago and out of gratitude sleeps with her plastic surgeon every third Wednesday.

"Oh, good," Charity says. "I'm glad you're back early. I need to talk."

She's been writing checks. MCI, Con Ed, Bonwit Teller. Envelopes, already stamped and sealed, form a pyramid between her shapely, knee-socked legs. The checkbook's cover is brown plastic, grained to look like cowhide. Each time Charity flips back the cover, white geese fly over sky-colored checks. She makes good money, but she's extravagant. The difference adds up to this shared, rent-controlled Chelsea one-bedroom.

"All right. Talk."

When I first moved in, she was seeing an analyst. Now she sees a nutritionist.

"Eric called. From Oregon."

"What did he want?"

"He wants me to pay half the rent on his loft for last spring. He asked me to move back, remember? He *begged* me."

Eric is Charity's estranged husband.

"What does your nutritionist say?" Eric now wears a red jumpsuit and tills the soil in Rajneeshpuram.

"You think Phil's a creep too, don't you? What else can he be when creeps are all I attract?"

Phil is a flutist with thinning hair. He's very touchy on the subject of *flautists* versus *flutists*. He's touchy on every subject, from music to books to foods to clothes. He teaches at a small college upstate, and Charity bought a used blue Datsun ("Nissan," Phil insists) last month so she could spend weekends with him. She returns every Sunday night, exhausted and exasperated. Phil and I don't have much to say to each other— he's the only musician I know; the men in my family are lawyers, engineers, or in business—but I like him. Around me, he loosens up. When he visits, he bakes us loaves of pumpernickel bread. He waxes our kitchen floor. Like many men in this country, he seems to me a displaced child, or even a woman, looking for something that passed him by, or for something that he can never have. If he thinks I'm not looking, he sneaks his hands under Charity's sweater, but there isn't too much there. Here, she's a model with high ambitions. In India, she'd be a flat-chested old maid.

I'm shy in front of the lovers. A darkness comes over me when I see them horsing around.

"It isn't the money," Charity says. Oh? I think. "He says he still loves me. Then he turns around and asks me for five hundred."

What's so strange about that, I want to ask. She still loves Eric, and Eric, red jump suit and all, is smart enough to know it. Love is a commodity, hoarded like any other. Mamet knows. But I say, "I'm not the person to ask about love." Charity knows that mine was a traditional Hindu marriage. My parents, with the help of a marriage broker, who was my mother's cousin, picked out a groom. All I had to do was get to know his taste in food.

It'll be a long evening, I'm afraid. Charity likes to confess. I unpleat my silk sari—it no longer looks too showy—wrap it in muslin cloth and put it away in a dresser drawer. Saris are hard to have laundered in Manhattan, though there's a good man in Jackson Heights. My next step will be to brew us a pot of chrysanthemum tea. It's a very special tea from the mainland. Charity's uncle gave it to us. I like him. He's a humpbacked, awkward, terrified man. He runs a gift store on Mott Street, and though he doesn't speak much English, he seems to have done well. Once upon a time he worked for the railways in Chengdu, Szechwan Province, and during the Wuchang Uprising, he was shot at. When I'm down, when I'm lonely for my husband, when I think of our son, or when I need to be held, I think of Charity's uncle. If I hadn't left home, I'd never have heard of the Wuchang Uprising. I've broadened my horizons.

Very late that night my husband calls me from Ahmadabad, a town of textile mills north of Bombay. My husband is a vice president at Lakshmi Cotton Mills. Lakshmi is the goddess of wealth, but LCM (Priv.), Ltd., is doing poorly. Lockouts, strikes, rock-throwings. My husband lives on digitalis, which he calls the food for our *yuga* of discontent.

"We had a bad mishap at the mill today." Then he says nothing for seconds.

The operator comes on. "Do you have the right party, sir? We're trying to reach Mrs. Butt."

"Bhatt," I insist. "*B* for Bombay, *H* for Haryana, *A* for Ahmadabad, double *T* for Tamil Nadu." It's a litany. "This is she."

"One of our lorries was firebombed today. Resulting in three deaths. The driver, old Karamchand, and his two children."

I know how my husband's eyes look this minute, how the eye rims sag and the yellow corneas shine and bulge with pain. He is not an emotional man—the Ahmadabad Institute of Management has trained him to cut losses, to look on the bright side of economic catastrophes—but tonight he's feeling low. I try to remember a driver named Karamchand, but can't. That part of my life is over, the way *trucks* have replaced *lorries* in my vocabulary, the way Charity Chin and her lurid love life have replaced inherited notions of marital duty. Tomorrow he'll come out of it. Soon he'll be eating again. He'll sleep like a baby. He's been trained to believe in turnovers. Every morning he rubs his scalp with cantharidine oil so his hair will grow back again.

"It could be your car next." Affection, love. Who can tell the difference in a traditional marriage in which a wife still doesn't call her husband by his first name?

"No. They know I'm a flunky, just like them. Well paid, maybe. No need for undue anxiety, please."

Then his voice breaks. He says he needs me, he misses me, he wants me to come to him damp from my evening shower, smelling of sandalwood soap, my braid decorated with jasmines.

"I need you too."

"Not to worry, please," he says. "I am coming in a fortnight's time. I have already made arrangements."

Outside my window, fire trucks whine, up Eighth Avenue. I wonder if he can hear them, what he thinks of a life like mine, led amid disorder.

"I am thinking it'll be like a honeymoon. More or less."

When I was in college, waiting to be married, I imagined honeymoons were only for the more fashionable girls, the girls who came from slightly racy families, smoked Sobranies in the dorm lavatories and put up posters of Kabir Bedi, who was supposed to have made it as a big star in the West. My husband wants us to go to Niagara. I'm not to worry about foreign exchange. He's arranged for extra dollars through the Gujarati Network, with a cousin in San Jose. And he's bought four hundred more on the black market. "Tell me you need me. Panna, please tell me again."

I change out of the cotton pants and shirt I've been wearing all day and put on a sari to meet my husband at JFK. I don't forget the jewelry; the marriage necklace of *mangalsutra*, gold drop earrings, heavy gold bangles. I don't wear them every day. In this borough of vice and greed, who knows when, or whom, desire will overwhelm.

My husband spots me in the crowd and waves. He has lost weight, and changed his glasses. The arm, uplifted in a cheery wave, is bony, frail, almost opalescent.

In the Carey Coach, we hold hands. He strokes my fingers one by one. "How come you aren't wearing my mother's ring?"

"Because muggers know about Indian women," I say. They know with us it's 24-karat. His mother's ring is showy, in ghastly taste anywhere but India: a blood-red Burma ruby set in a gold frame of floral sprays. My mother-in-law got her guru to bless the ring before I left for the States.

He looks disconcerted. He's used to a different role. He's the knowing, suspicious one in the family. He seems to be sulking, and finally he comes out with it. "You've said nothing about my new glasses." I compliment him on the glasses, how chic and Western-executive they make him look. But I can't help the other things, necessities until he learns the ropes. I handle the money, buy the tickets. I don't know if this makes me unhappy.

Charity drives her Nissan upstate, so for two weeks we are to have the apartment to ourselves. This is more privacy than we ever had in India. No parents, no servants, to keep us modest. We play at housekeeping. Imre has lent us a hibachi, and I grill saffron chicken breasts. My husband marvels at the size of the Perdue hens. "They're big like peacocks, no? These Americans, they're really something!" He tries out pizzas, burgers, McNuggets. He chews. He explores. He judges. He loves it all, fears nothing, feels at home in the summer odors, the clutter of Manhattan streets. Since he thinks that the American palate is bland, he carries a bottle of red peppers in his pocket. I wheel a shopping cart down the aisles of the neighborhood Grand Union, and he follows, swiftly, greedily. He picks up hair rinses and high-protein diet powders. There's so much I already take for granted.

One night, Imre stops by. He wants us to go with him to a movie. In his work shirt and red leather tie, he looks arty or strung out. It's only been a week, but I feel as though I am really seeing him for the first time. The yellow hair worn very short at the sides, the wide, narrow lips. He's a good-looking man, but self-conscious, almost arrogant. He's picked the movie we should see. He always tells me what to see, what to read. He buys the *Voice*. He's a natural avant-gardist. For tonight he's chosen *Numéro Deux*.

"Is it a musical?" my husband asks. The Radio City Music Hall is on his list of sights to see. He's read up on the history of the Rockettes. He doesn't catch Imre's sympathetic wink.

Guilt, shame, loyalty. I long to be ungracious, not ingratiate myself with both men.

That night my husband calculates in rupees the money we've wasted on Godard. "That refugee fellow, Nagy, must have a screw loose in his head. I paid very steep price for dollars on the black market."

Some afternoons we go shopping. Back home we hated shopping, but now it is a lovers' project. My husband's shopping list startles me. I feel I am just getting to know him. Maybe, like Imre, freed from the dignities of old-world culture, he too could get drunk and squirt Cheez Whiz on a guest. I watch him dart into stores in his gleaming leather shoes. Jockey shorts on sale in outdoor bins on Broadway entrance him. White tube socks with different bands of color delight him. He looks for microcassettes, for anything small and electronic and smuggleable. He needs a garment bag. He calls it a "wardrobe," and I have to translate.

"All of New York is having sales, no?"

My heart speeds watching him this happy. It's the third week in August, almost the end of summer, and the city smells ripe, it cannot bear more heat, more money, more energy.

"This is so smashing! The prices are so excellent!" Recklessly, my prudent husband signs away traveller's checks. How he intends to smuggle it all back I don't dare ask. With a microwave, he calculates, we could get rid of our cook.

This has to be love, I think. Charity, Eric, Phil: they may be experts on sex. My husband doesn't chase me around the sofa, but he pushes me down on Charity's battered cushions, and the man who has never entered the kitchen of our Ahmadabad house now comes toward me with a dish tub of steamy water to massage away the pavement heat.

Ten days into his vacation my husband checks out brochures for sightseeing tours. Shortline, Grayline, Crossroads: his new vinyl briefcase is full of schedules and pamphlets. While I make pancakes out of a mix, he comparison-shops. Tour number one costs $10.95 and will give us the World Trade Center, Chinatown, and the United Nations. Tour number three would take us both uptown *and* downtown for $14.95, but my husband is absolutely sure he doesn't want to see Harlem. We settle for tour number four: Downtown and the Dame. It's offered by a new tour company with a small, dirty office at Eighth and Forty-eighth.

The sidewalk outside the office is colorful with tourists. My husband sends me in to buy the tickets because he has come to feel Americans don't understand his accent.

The dark man, Lebanese probably, behind the counter comes on too friendly. "Come on, doll, make my day!" He won't say which tour is his. "Number four? Honey, no! Look, you've wrecked me! Say you'll change your mind." He takes two twenties and gives back change. He holds the tickets, forcing me to pull. He leans closer. "I'm off after lunch."

My husband must have been watching me from the sidewalk. "What was the chap saying?" he demands. "I told you not to wear pants. He thinks you are Puerto Rican. He thinks he can treat you with disrespect."

The bus is crowded and we have to sit across the aisle from each other. The tour guide begins his patter on Forty-sixth. He looks like an actor, his hair bleached and blow-dried. Up close he must look middle-aged, but from where I sit his skin is smooth and his cheeks faintly red.

"Welcome to the Big Apple, folks." The guide uses a microphone. "Big Apple. That's what we native Manhattan degenerates call our city. Today we have guests from fifteen foreign countries and six states from this U.S. of A. That makes the Tourist Bureau real happy. And let me assure you that while we may be the richest city in the richest country in the world, it's okay to tip your charming and talented attendant." He laughs. Then he swings his hip out into the aisle and sings a song.

"And it's mighty fancy on old Delancey Street, you know. . . ."

My husband looks irritable. The guide is, as expected, a good singer. "The bloody man should be giving us histories of buildings we are passing, no?" I pat his hand, the mood passes. He cranes his neck. Our window seats have both gone to Japanese. It's the tour of his life. Next to this, the quick business trips to Manchester and Glasgow pale.

"And tell me what street compares to Mott Street, in July. . . ."

The guide wants applause. He manages a derisive laugh from the Americans up front. He's working the aisles now. "I coulda been somebody, right? I coulda been a star!" Two or three of us smile, those of us who recognize the parody. He catches my smile. The sun is on his harsh, bleached hair. "Right, your highness? Look, we gotta maharani with us! Couldn't I have been a star?"

"Right!" I say, my voice coming out a squeal. I've been trained to adapt; what else can I say?

We drive through traffic past landmark office buildings and

churches. The guide flips his hands. "Art deco," he keeps saying. I hear him confide to one of the Americans: "Beats me. I went to a cheap guide's school." My husband wants to know more about this Art Deco, but the guide sings another song.

"We made a foolish choice," my husband grumbles. "We are sitting in the bus only. We're not going into famous buildings." He scrutinizes the pamphlets in his jacket pocket. I think, at least it's air-conditioned in here. I could sit here in the cool shadows of the city forever.

Only five of us appear to have opted for the "Downtown and the Dame" tour. The others will ride back uptown past the United Nations after we've been dropped off at the pier for the ferry to the Statue of Liberty.

An elderly European pulls a camera out of his wife's designer tote bag. He takes pictures of the boats in the harbor, the Japanese in kimonos eating popcorn, scavenging pigeons, me. Then, pushing his wife ahead of him, he climbs back on the bus and waves to us. For a second I feel terribly lost. I wish we were on the bus going back to the apartment. I know I'll not be able to describe any of this to Charity, or to Imre. I'm too proud to admit I went on a guided tour.

The view of the city from the Circle Line ferry is seductive, unreal. The skyline wavers out of reach, but never quite vanishes. The summer sun pushes through fluffy clouds and dapples the glass of office towers. My husband looks thrilled, even more than he had on the shopping trips down Broadway. Tourists and dreamers, we have spent our life's savings to see this skyline, this statue.

"Quick, take a picture of me!" my husband yells as he moves toward a gap of railings. A Japanese matron has given up her position in order to change film. "Before the Twin Towers disappear!"

I focus, I wait for a large Oriental family to walk out of my range. My husband holds his pose tight against the railing. He wants to look relaxed, an international businessman at home in all the financial markets.

A bearded man slides across the bench toward me. "Like this," he says and helps me get my husband in focus. "You want me to take the photo for you?" His name, he says, is Goran. He is Goran from Yugoslavia, as though that were enough for tracking him down. Imre from Hungary. Panna from India. He pulls the old Leica out of my hand, signaling the Orientals to beat it, and clicks away. "I'm a photographer," he says. He could have been a camera thief. That's what my husband would have assumed. Somehow, I trusted. "Get you a beer?" he asks.

"I don't. Drink, I mean. Thank you very much." I say those last words very loud, for everyone's benefit. The odd bottles of Soave with Imre don't count.

"Too bad." Goran gives back the camera.

"Take one more!" my husband shouts from the railing. "Just to be sure!"

The island itself disappoints. The Lady has brutal scaffolding holding her in. The museum is closed. The snack bar is dirty and expensive. My husband reads out the prices to me. He orders two french fries and two Cokes. We sit at picnic tables and wait for the ferry to take us back.

"What was that hippie chap saying?"

As if I could say. A day-care center has brought its kids, at least forty of them, to the island for the day. The kids, all wearing name tags, run around us. I can't help noticing how many are Indian. Even a Patel, probably a Bhatt if I looked hard enough. They toss hamburger bits at pigeons. They kick styrofoam cups. The pigeons are slow, greedy, persistent. I have to shoo one off the table top. I don't think my husband thinks about our son.

"What hippie?"

"The one on the boat. With the beard and the hair."

My husband doesn't look at me. He shakes out his paper napkin and tries to protect his french fries from pigeon feathers.

"Oh, him. He said he was from Dubrovnik." It isn't true, but I don't want trouble.

"What did he say about Dubrovnik?"

I know enough about Dubrovnik to get by. Imre's told me about it. And about Mostar and Zagreb. In Mostar white Muslims sing the call to prayer. I would like to see that before I die: white Muslims. Whole peoples have moved before me; they've adapted. The night Imre told me about Mostar was also the night I saw my first snow in Manhattan. We'd walked down to Chelsea from Columbia. We'd walked and talked and I hadn't felt tired at all.

"You're too innocent," my husband says. He reaches for my hand. "Panna," he cries with pain in his voice, and I am brought back from perfect, floating memories of snow, "I've come to take you back. I have seen how men watch you."

"What?"

"Come back, now. I have tickets. We have all the things we will ever need. I can't live without you."

A little girl with wiry braids kicks a bottle cap at his shoes. The pigeons wheel and scuttle around us. My husband covers his fries with spread-out fingers. "No kicking," he tells the girl. Her name, Beulah, is printed in green ink on a heart-shaped name tag. He forces a smile, and Beulah smiles back. Then she starts to flap her arms. She flaps, she hops. The pigeons go crazy for fries and scraps.

"Special ed. course is two years," I remind him. "I can't go back."

My husband picks up our trays and throws them into the garbage before I can stop him. He's carried disposability a little too far. "We've been taken," he says, moving toward the dock, though the ferry will not arrive for another twenty minutes. "The ferry costs only two dollars round-trip per person. We should have chosen tour number one for $10.95 instead of tour number four for $14.95."

With my Lebanese friend, I think. "But this way we don't have to worry about cabs. The bus will pick us up at the pier and take us back to midtown. Then we can walk home."

"New York is full of cheats and whatnot. Just like Bombay." He is not accusing me of infidelity. I feel dread all the same.

That night, after we've gone to bed, the phone rings. My husband listens, then hands the phone to me. "What is this woman saying?" He turns on the pink Macy's lamp by the bed. "I am not understanding these Negro people's accents."

The operator repeats the message. It's a cable from one of the directors of Lakshmi Cotton Mills. "Massive violent labor confrontation anticipated. Stop. Return posthaste. Stop. Cable flight details. Signed Kantilal Shah."

"It's not your factory," I say. "You're supposed to be on vacation."

"So, you are worrying about me? Yes? You reject my heartfelt wishes but you worry about me?" He pulls me close, slips the straps of my nightdress off my shoulder. "Wait a minute."

I wait, unclothed, for my husband to come back to me. The water is running in the bathroom. In the ten days he has been here he has learned American rites: deodorants, fragrances. Tomorrow morning he'll call Air India; tomorrow evening he'll be on his way back to Bombay. Tonight I should make up to him for my years away, the gutted trucks, the degree I'll never use in India. I want to pretend with him that nothing has changed.

In the mirror that hangs on the bathroom door, I watch my naked body turn, the breasts, the thighs glow. The body's beauty amazes. I stand here shameless, in ways he has never seen me. I am free, afloat, watching somebody else.

LOOSE
ENDS

S HE sends for this Goldilocks doll in April.

"See," she says. The magazine is pressed tight to her T-shirt. "It's porcelain."

I look. The ad calls Goldilocks "the first doll in an enchanting new suite of fairy tale dolls."

"*Bisque* porcelain," she says. She fills out the order form in purple ink. "Look at the pompoms on her shoes. Aren't they darling?"

"You want to blow sixty bucks?" Okay, so I yell that at Jonda. "You have any idea how much I got to work for sixty dollars?"

"Only twenty now," she says. Then she starts bitching. "What's with you and Velásquez these days? You shouldn't even be home in the afternoon."

It's between one and two and I have a right, don't I, to be in my Manufactured Home—as they call it—in Laguna Vista Estates instead of in Mr. Vee's pastel office in the mall? A man's mobile home is his castle, at least in Florida. But I fix her her bourbon and ginger ale with the dash of ReaLemon just the way she likes it. She isn't a mail-order junky; this Goldilocks thing is more complicated.

"It makes me nervous," Jonda goes on. "To have you home, I mean."

I haven't been fired by Mr. Vee; the truth is I've been offered a raise, contingent, of course, on my delivering a forceful message to that greaser goon, Chavez. I don't get into that with Jonda. Jonda doesn't have much of a head for details.

"Learn to like it," I say. "Your boyfriend better learn, too."

She doesn't have anyone but me, but she seems to like the jealousy bit. Her face goes soft and dreamy like the old days. We've seen a lot together.

"Jonda," I start. I just don't get it. What does she want?

"Forget it, Jeb." She licks the stamp on the Goldilocks envelope so gooey it sticks on crooked. "There's no point in us talking. We don't communicate anymore."

I make myself a cocktail. Milk, two ice cubes crushed with a hammer between two squares of paper towel, and Maalox. Got the recipe from a NamVets magazine.

"Look at you." She turns on the TV and gets in bed. "I hate to see you like this, at loose ends."

I get in bed with her. Usually afternoons are pure dynamite, when I can get them. I lie down with her for a while, but nothing happens. We're like that until Oprah comes on.

"It's okay," Jonda says. "I'm going to the mall. The guy who opened the new boutique, you know, the little guy with the turban, he said he might be hiring."

I drop a whole ice cube into my Maalox cocktail and watch her change. She shimmies out of khaki shorts—mementoes of my glory days—and pulls a flowery skirt over her head. I still don't feel any urge.

"Who let these guys in?" I say. She doesn't answer. He won't hire her—they come in with half a dozen kids and pay them nothing. We're coolie labor in our own country.

She pretends to look for her car keys which are hanging as usual from their nail. "Don't wait up for me."

"At least let me drive you." I'm not begging, yet.

"No, it's okay." She fixes her wickedly green eyes on me. And suddenly bile pours out in torrents. "Nine years, for God's sake! Nine years, and what do we have?"

"Don't let's get started."

Hey, what we have sounds like the Constitution of the United States. We have freedom and no strings attached. We have no debts. We come and go as we like. She wants a kid but I don't think I have the makings of a good father. That's part of what the Goldilocks thing is.

But I know what she means. By the time Goldilocks arrives in the mail, she'll have moved her stuff out of Laguna Vista Estates.

I like Miami. I like the heat. You can smell the fecund rot of the jungle in every headline. You can park your car in the shopping mall and watch the dope change hands, the Goldilockses and Peter Pans go off with new daddies, the dishwashers and short-order cooks haggle over fake passports, the Mr. Vees in limos huddle over arms-shopping lists, all the while gull guano drops on your car with the soothing steadiness of rain.

Don't get me wrong. I liked the green spaces of Nam, too. In spite of the consequences. I was the Pit Bull—even the Marines backed off. I was Jesse James hunched tight in the gunship, trolling the jungle for hidden wonders.

"If you want to stay alive," Doc Healy cautioned me the first day, "just keep consuming and moving like a locust. Do that, Jeb m'boy, and you'll survive to die a natural death." Last winter a judge put a vet away for thirty-five years for sinking his teeth into sweet, succulent coed flesh. The judge said, *when gangrene sets in, the doctor has no choice but to amputate.* But I'm here to testify, Your Honor, the appetite remains, after the easy targets have all been eaten. The whirring of our locust jaws is what keeps you awake.

I take care of Chavez for Mr. Vee and come home to stale tangled sheets. Jonda's been gone nine days.

I'm not whining. Last night in the parking lot of the mall a swami with blond dreadlocks treated us to a levitation. We spied him on the roof of a discount clothing store, nudging his flying mat into liftoff position. We were the usual tourists and weirdos and murderous cubanos. First he played his sinuses OM-OOM-OOMPAH-OOM, then he pushed off from the roof in the lotus position. His bare feet sprouted like orchids from his knees. We watched him wheel and flutter for maybe two or three minutes before the cops pulled up and caught him in a safety net.

They took him away in handcuffs. Who knows how many killers and felons and honest nut cases watched it and politely went back to their cars? I love Miami.

This morning I lean on Mr. Vee's doorbell. I need money. Auguste, the bouncer he picked up in the back streets of Montreal, squeezes my windbreaker before letting me in.

I suck in my gut and make the palm trees on my shirt ripple. "You're blonder than you were. Blond's definitely your color."

"Don't start with me, Marshall," he says. He helps himself to a mint from a fancy glass bowl on the coffee table.

Mr. Vee sidles into the room; he's one hundred and seventy-five pounds of jiggling paranoia.

"You look like hell, Marshall," is the first thing he says.

"I could say the same to you, Haysoos," I say.

His face turns mean. I scoop up a mint and flip it like a quarter.

"The last job caused me some embarrassment," he says.

My job, I try to remind him, is to show up at a time and place of his choosing and perform a simple operation. I'm the gunship Mr. Vee calls in. He pinpoints the target, I attempt to neutralize it. It's all a matter of instrumentation and precise coordinates. With more surveillance, a longer lead time, a neutral setting, mishaps can be minimized. But not on the money Mr. Vee pays. He's itchy and impulsive; he wants a quick hit, publicity, and some sort of ego boost. I served under second looies just like him, and sooner or later most of them got blown away, after losing half their men.

The story was, Chavez had been sampling too much of Mr. Vee's product line. He was, as a result, inoperative with women. He lived in a little green house in a postwar development on the fringes of Liberty City, a step up, in some minds, from a trailer park. By all indications, he should have been alone. I get a little sick when wives and kids are involved, old folks, neighbors, repairmen—I'm not a monster, except when I'm being careful.

I gained entry through a window—thank God for cheap air conditioners. First surprise: he wasn't alone. I could hear that drug-deep double-breathing. Even in the dark before I open a door, I can tell a woman from a man, middle age from adolescence, a sleeping Cuban from a sleeping American. They were entwined; it looked like at long last love for poor old Chavez. She might have been fourteen, brassy-haired with wide black roots, baby-fat-bodied with a pinched, Appalachian face. I did what I was paid for; I eliminated the primary target and left no traces. Doc Healy used to teach us: torch the whole hut and make sure you get the kids, the grannies, cringing on the sleeping mat—or else you'll meet them on the trail with fire in their eyes.

Truth be told, I was never much of a marksman. My game is getting close, working the body, where accuracy doesn't count for much. We're the guys who survived that war.

The carnage at Chavez's cost me, too. You get a reputation, especially if young women are involved. You don't look so good anymore to sweatier clients.

I lean over and flick an imaginary fruit fly off Haysoos Velásquez's shiny lapel. Auguste twitches.

"What did you do that for?" he shrieks.

"I could get you deported real easy." I smile. I want him to know that for all his flash and jangle and elocution lessons so he won't go around like an underworld Ricky Ricardo, to me he's just another boat person. "You got something good for me today?"

A laugh leaks out of him. "You're so burned out, Marshall,

you couldn't fuck a whore." He extracts limp bills from a safe. Two thousand to blow town for a while, till it cools.

"*Gracias, amigo.*" At least this month the trailer's safe, if not the car. Which leaves me free to hotwire a newer model.

Where did America go? I want to know. Down the rabbit hole, Doc Healy used to say. Alice knows, but she took it with her. Hard to know which one's the Wonderland. Back when me and my buddies were barricading the front door, who left the back door open?

And just look at what Alice left behind.

She left behind a pastel house, lime-sherbet color, a little south and a little west of Miami, with sprinklers batting water across a yard the size of a badminton court. In the back bedroom there's a dripping old air conditioner. The window barely closes over it. It's an old development, they don't have outside security, wire fences, patrol dogs. It's a retirement bungalow like they used to advertise in the comic pages of the Sunday papers. No one was around in those days to warn the old folks that the lots hadn't quite surfaced from the slime, and the soil was too salty to take a planting. And twenty years later there'd still be that odor—gamey, fishy, sour rot—of a tropical city on unrinsed water, where the blue air shimmers with diesel fumes and the gray water thickens like syrup from saturated waste.

Chavez, stewing in his juices.

And when your mammy and pappy die off and it's time to sell off the lime-sherbet bungalow, who's there to buy it? A nice big friendly greaser like Mr. Chavez.

Twenty years ago I missed the meaning of things around me. I was seventeen years old, in Heidelberg, Germany, about to be shipped out to Vietnam. We had guys on the base selling passages to Sweden. And I had a weekend pass and a free flight to London. Held them in my hand: Sweden forever, or a weekend pass. Wise up, kid, choose life, whispered the cook, a twenty-year lifer with a quarter million stashed in Arizona.

Seventeen years old and guys are offering me life or death, only I didn't see it then.

When you're a teenage buckaroo from Ocala, Florida, in London for the first time, where do you go? I went to the London Zoo. Okay, so I was a kid checking out the snakes and gators of my childhood. You learn to love a languid, ugly target.

I found myself in front of the reticulated python. This was one huge serpent. It squeezed out jaguars and crocodiles like dishrags. It was twenty-eight feet long and as thick as my waist, with a snout as long and wide as a croc's. The *scale* of the thing was beyond impressive, beyond incredible. If you ever want to feel helpless or see what the odds look like when they're stacked against you, imagine the embrace of the reticulated python. The tip of its tail at the far end of the concrete pool could have been in a different county. Its head was out of water, resting on the tub's front edge. The head is what got me, that broad, patient, intelligent face, those eyes brown and passionless as all of Vietnam.

Dead rabbits were plowed in a corner. I felt nothing for the bunnies.

Then I noticed the snakeshit. Python turds, dozens of turds, light as cork and thick as a tree, riding high in the water. Once you'd seen them, you couldn't help thinking you'd smelled them all along. *That's* what I mean about Florida, about all the hot-water ports like Bangkok, Manila and Bombay, living on water where the shit's so thick it's a kind of cash crop.

Behind me, one of those frosty British matrons whispered to her husband, "I didn't know they *did* such things!"

"Believe it, Queenie," I said.

That snakeshit—all that coiled power—stays with me, always. That's what happened to us in the paddyfields. We drowned in our shit. An inscrutable humanoid python sleeping on a bed of turds: that's what I never want to be.

So I keep two things in mind nowadays. First, Florida was built for your pappy and grammie. I remember them, I was a kid here, I remember the good Florida when only the pioneers came down and it was considered too hot and wet and buggy to ever come to much. I knew your pappy and grammie, I mowed their lawn, trimmed their hedges, washed their cars. I toted their golf bags. Nice people—they deserved a few years of golf, a garden to show off when their kids came down to visit, a white car that justified its extravagant air conditioning and never seemed to get dirty. That's the first thing about Florida; the nice thing. The second is this: Florida is run by locusts and behind them are sharks and even pythons and they've pretty well chewed up your mom and pop and all the other lawn bowlers and blue-haired ladies. On the outside, life goes on in Florida courtesy of middlemen who bring in things that people are willing to pay a premium to obtain.

Acapulco, Tijuana, Freeport, Miami—it doesn't matter where the pimping happens. Mr. Vee in his nostalgic moments tells me Havana used to be like that, a city of touts and pimps— the fat young men in sunglasses parked at a corner in an idling Buick, waiting for a payoff, a delivery, a contact. Havana has shifted its corporate headquarters. Beirut has come west. And now, it's Miami that gives me warm memories of always-Christmas Saigon.

It's life in the procurement belt, between those lines of tropical latitudes, where the world shops for its illicit goods and dumps its surplus parts, where it prefers to fight its wars, and once you've settled into its give and take, you find it's impossible to live anywhere else. It's the coke-and-caffeine jangle of being seventeen and readier to kill than be killed and to know that Job One is to secure your objective and after that it's unsupervised play till the next order comes down.

In this mood, and in a Civic newly liberated from a protesting coed, I am heading west out of Miami, thinking first of driving up to Pensacola when I am sideswiped off the highway. Two men get in the Civic. They sit on either side of me and light up cigarettes.

"Someone say something," I finally say.

They riffle through the papers in the glove compartment. They quickly surmise that my name is not Mindy Robles. "We know all about this morning. Assault. Grand theft auto."

"Let's talk," I say.

I wait for the rough stuff. When it comes, it's an armlock on the throat that cuts air supply. When they let me speak, I cut a deal. They spot me for a vet; we exchange some dates, names, firefights. Turns out they didn't like Mindy Robles, didn't appreciate the pressure her old man tried to put on the police department. They look at our names—Robles and Marshall—and I can read their minds. We're in some of these things together and no one's linked me to Chávez—these guys are small time, auto-detail. They keep the car. They filch a wad of Mr. Vee's bills, the wad I'd stuffed into my wallet. They don't know there's another wad of Mr. Vee's money in a secret place. And fifty bucks in my boots.

Instead of an air-conditioned nighttime run up the Gulf coast, it's the thumb on the interstate. I pass up a roadside rest area, a happy hunting ground for new cars and ready cash. I hitch a ride to the farthest cheap motel.

The first automobile I crouch behind in the dark parking lot of the Dunes Motel is an Impala with Alabama license plates. The next one is Broward County. Two more out-of-staters: Live Free or Die and Land of Lincoln. The farther from Florida the better for me. I look in the windows of the Topaz from New Hampshire. There's a rug in the back seat, and under the rug I make out a shiny sliver of Samsonite. Maybe they're just eating. Clothes hang on one side: two sports jackets for a small man or an adolescent, and what looks to me like lengths of silk. On the rear-view mirror, where you or I might hang a kid's booties or a plastic Jesus and rosaries, is an alien deity with four arms or legs. I don't know about borrowing this little beauty. These people travel a little too heavy.

The Dunes isn't an absolute dump. The pool has water in it. The neon VACANCY sign above the door of the office has blown only one letter. The annex to the left of the office has its own separate entrance: SANDALWOOD RESTAURANT.

I stroke the highway dust out of my hair, so the office won't guess my present automobileless state, tuck my shirt into my Levis and walk in from the parking lot. The trouble is there's nobody behind the desk. It's 11:03; late but not late enough for even a junior high jailbait nightclerk to have taken to her cot.

Another guest might have rung the bell and waited, or rung the bell and banged his fist on the counter and done some swearing. What I do is count on the element of surprise. I vault into the staff area and kick open a door that says: STRICTLY PRIVATE.

Inside, in a room reeking of incense, are people eating. There are a lot of them. There are a lot of little brown people sitting cross-legged on the floor of a regular motel room and eating with their hands. Pappies with white beards, grammies swaddled in silk, men in dark suits, kids, and one luscious jailbait in blue jeans.

They look at me. A bunch of aliens and they stare like I'm the freak.

One of the aliens tries to uncross his legs, but all he manages is a backward flop. He holds his right hand stiff and away from his body so it won't drip gravy on his suit. "Are you wanting a room?"

I've never liked the high, whiny Asian male voice. "Let's put it this way. Are you running a motel or what?"

The rest of the aliens look at me, look at each other, look down at their food. I stare at them too. They seem to have been partying. I wouldn't mind a Jack Daniels and a plate of their rice and yellow stew stuff brought to me by room service in blue jeans.

"Some people here say we are running a 'po-tel'." A greasy grin floats off his face. "Get it? My name is Patel, that's P-A-T-E-L. A Patel owning a motel, get it?"

"Rich," I say.

The jailbait springs up off the floor. With a gecko-fast tongue tip, she chases a gravy drop on her wrist. "I can go. I'm done." But she doesn't make a move. "You people enjoy the meal."

The women jabber, but not in English. They flash gold bracelets. An organized raid could clean up in that room, right down to the rubies and diamonds in their noses. They're all wrapped in silk, like brightly-colored mummies. Pappy shakes his head, but doesn't rise. "She eats like a bird. Who'll marry her?" he says in English to one of his buddies.

"You should advertise," says the other man, probably the Living Free or Dying. They've forgotten me. I feel left out, left behind. While we were nailing up that big front door, these guys were sneaking in around back. They got their money, their family networks, and their secretive languages.

I verbalize a little seething, and when none of the aliens take notice, I dent the prefab wall with my fist. "Hey," I yell. "I need a room for the night. Don't any of you dummies speak American?"

Now she swings toward me apologetically. She has a braid that snakes all the way down to her knees. "Sorry for the inconvenience," she says. She rinses gravy off her hands. "It's our biggest family reunion to date. That's why things are so hectic." She says something about a brother getting married, leaving them short at the desk. I think of Jonda and the turbaned guy. He fired her when some new turbaned guy showed up.

"Let's just go," I say. "I don't give a damn about reunions." I don't know where Jonda ended up. The Goldilocks doll wasn't delivered to Laguna Vista Estates, though I had a welcome planned for it.

This kid's got a ripe body. I follow the ripe body up a flight of outdoor stairs. Lizards scurry, big waterbugs drag across the landings.

"This is it," she says. She checks the air conditioning and the TV. She makes sure there are towels in the bathroom. If she feels a little uneasy being in a motel room with a guy like me who's dusty and scruffy and who kills for a living, she doesn't show it. Not till she looks back at the door and realizes I'm not carrying any bags.

She's a pro. "You'll have to pay in cash now," she says. "I'll make out a receipt."

"What if I were to pull out a knife instead," I joke. I turn slightly away from her and count the balance of Haysoos's bills. Not enough in there, after the shakedown. The fifty stays put, my new nest egg. "Where were you born, honey? Bombay? I been to Bombay."

"New Jersey," she says. "You can pay half tonight, and the rest before you check out tomorrow. I am not unreasonable."

"I'll just bet you're not. Neither am I. But who says I'm leaving tomorrow. You got some sort of policy?"

That's when I catch the look on her face. Disgust, isn't that what it is? Distaste for the likes of me.

"You can discuss that with my father and uncle tomorrow morning." She sashays just out of my reach. She's aiming to race back to the motel room not much different than this except that it's jammed with family.

I pounce on Alice before she can drop down below, and take America with her. The hardware comes in handy, especially the kris. Alice lays hot fingers on my eyes and nose, but it's no use and once she knows it, Alice submits.

I choose me the car with the Land of Lincoln plates. I make a double switch with Broward County. I drive the old Tamiami Trail across the remains of the Everglades. Used to be no cars, a narrow ridge of two-lane concrete with swamps on either side, gators sunning themselves by day, splattered by night. Black snakes and mocassins every few hundred yards. Clouds of mosquitoes.

This is what I've become. I want to squeeze this state dry and swallow it whole.

ORBITING

ON Thanksgiving morning I'm still in my nightgown thinking of Vic when Dad raps on my apartment door. Who's he rolling joints for, who's he initiating now into the wonders of his inner space? What got me on Vic is remembering last Thanksgiving and his famous cranberry sauce with Grand Marnier, which Dad had interpreted as a sign of permanence in my life. A man who cooks like Vic is ready for other commitments. Dad cannot imagine cooking as self-expression. You cook *for* someone. Vic's sauce was a sign of his permanent isolation, if you really want to know.

Dad's come to drop off the turkey. It's a seventeen-pounder. Mr. Vitelli knows to reserve a biggish one for us every Thanksgiving and Christmas. But this November what with Danny in the Marines, Uncle Carmine having to be very careful after the bypass, and Vic taking off for outer space as well, we might as well have made do with one of those turkey rolls you pick out of the freezer. And in other years, Mr. Vitelli would not have given us a frozen bird. We were proud of that, our birds were fresh killed. I don't bring this up to Dad.

"Your mama took care of the thawing," Dad says. "She said you wouldn't have room in your Frigidaire."

"You mean Mom said Rindy shouldn't be living in a dump,

57

right?" Mom has the simple, immigrant faith that children should do better than their parents, and her definition of better is comfortingly rigid. Fair enough—I believed it, too. But the fact is all I can afford is this third-floor studio with an art deco shower. The fridge fits under the kitchenette counter. The room has potential. I'm content with that. And I *like* my job even though it's selling, not designing, jewelry made out of seashells and semiprecious stones out of a boutique in Bellevue Plaza.

Dad shrugs. "You're an adult, Renata." He doesn't try to lower himself into one of my two deck chairs. He was a minor league catcher for a while and his knees went. The fake zebra-skin cushions piled as seats on the rug are out of the question for him. My futon bed folds up into a sofa, but the satin sheets are still lasciviously tangled. My father stands in a slat of sunlight, trying not to look embarrassed.

"Dad, I'd have come to the house and picked it up. You didn't have to make the extra trip out from Verona." A sixty-five-year-old man in wingtips and a Borsalino hugging a wet, heavy bird is so poignant I have to laugh.

"You wouldn't have gotten out of bed until noon, Renata." But Dad smiles. I know what he's saying. He's saying *he's* retired and *he* should be able to stay in bed till noon if he wants to, but he can't and he'd rather drive twenty miles with a soggy bird than read the *Ledger* one more time.

Grumbling and scolding are how we deMarcos express love. It's the North Italian way, Dad used to tell Cindi, Danny, and me when we were kids. Sicilians and Calabrians are emotional; we're contained. Actually, *he's* contained, the way Vic was contained for the most part. Mom's a Calabrian and she was born and raised there. Dad's very American, so Italy's a safe source of pride for him. I once figured it out: *his* father, Arturo deMarco, was a fifteen-week-old fetus when his mother planted her feet on Ellis Island. Dad, a proud son of North Italy had one big adventure in his life, besides fighting in the Pacific, and that was marrying a Calabrian peasant. He made it sound as though Mom was a Korean or something, and their marriage was a kind of taming of the West, and that everything about her could be explained as a cultural deficiency. Actually, Vic could talk beautifully about his feelings. He'd brew espresso, pour it into tiny blue pottery cups and analyze our relationship. I should have listened. I mean really listened. I thought he was talking about us, but I know now he was only talking incessantly about himself. I put too much faith in mail-order nightgowns and bras.

"Your mama wanted me out of the house," Dad goes on. "She didn't used to be like this, Renata."

Renata and Carla are what we were christened. We changed to Rindy and Cindi in junior high. Danny didn't have to make such leaps, unless you count dropping out of Montclair State and joining the Marines. He was always Danny, or Junior.

I lug the turkey to the kitchen sink where it can drip away at a crazy angle until I have time to deal with it.

"Your mama must have told you girls I've been acting funny since I retired."

"No, Dad, she hasn't said anything about you acting funny." What she *has* said is do we think she ought to call Doc Brunetti and have a chat about Dad? Dad wouldn't have to know. He and Doc Brunetti are, or were, on the same church league bowling team. So is, or was, Vic's dad, Vinny Riccio.

"Your mama thinks a man should have an office to drive to every day. I sat at a desk for thirty-eight years and what did I get? Ask Doc, I'm too embarrassed to say." Dad told me once Doc—his real name was Frankie, though no one ever called him that—had been called Doc since he was six years old and growing up with Dad in Little Italy. There was never a time in his life when Doc wasn't Doc, which made his professional decision very easy. Dad used to say, no one ever called me Adjuster when I was a kid. Why didn't they call me something like Sarge or Teach? Then I would have known better.

I wish I had something breakfasty in my kitchen cupboard to offer him. He wants to stay and talk about Mom, which is the way old married people have. Let's talk about me means: What do you think of Mom? I'll take the turkey over means: When will Rindy settle down? I wish this morning I had bought the Goodwill sofa for ten dollars instead of letting Vic haul off the fancy deck chairs from Fortunoff's. Vic had flash. He'd left Jersey a long time before he actually took off.

"I can make you tea."

"None of that herbal stuff."

We don't talk about Mom, but I know what he's going through. She's just started to find herself. He's not burned out, he's merely stuck. I remember when Mom refused to learn to drive, wouldn't leave the house even to mail a letter. Her litany those days was: when you've spent the first fifteen years of your life in a mountain village, when you remember candles and gaslight and carrying water from a well, not to mention holding in your water at night because of wolves and the unlit outdoor privy, you *like* being housebound. She used those wolves for all they were worth, as though imaginary wolves still nipped her heels in the Clifton Mall.

Before Mom began to find herself and signed up for a class at Paterson, she used to nag Cindi and me about finding the right men. "Men," she said; she wasn't coy, never. Unembarrassed, she'd tell me about her wedding night, about her first sighting of Dad's "thing" ("Land Ho!" Cindi giggled. "Thar she blows!" I chipped in.) and she'd giggle at our word for it, the common word, and she'd use it around us, never around Dad. Mom's peasant, she's earthy but never coarse. If I could get that across to Dad, how I admire it in men or in women, I would feel somehow redeemed of all my little mistakes with them, with men, with myself. Cindi and Brent were married on a cruise ship by the ship's captain. Tony, Vic's older brother, made a play for me my senior year. Tony's solid now. He manages a funeral home but he's invested in crayfish ponds on the side.

"You don't even own a dining table." Dad sounds petulant. He uses "even" a lot around me. Not just a judgment, but a comparative judgment. Other people have dining tables. *Lots* of dining tables. He softens it a bit, not wanting to hurt me, wanting more for me to judge him a failure. "We've always had a sit-down dinner, hon."

Okay, so traditions change. This year dinner's potluck. So I don't have real furniture. I eat off stack-up plastic tables as I watch the evening news. I drink red wine and heat a pita bread on the gas burner and wrap it around alfalfa sprouts or green linguine. The Swedish knockdown dresser keeps popping its sides because Vic didn't glue it properly. Swedish engineering, he said, doesn't need glue. Think of Volvos, he said, and Ingmar Bergman. He isn't good with directions that come in four languages. At least he wasn't.

"Trust me, Dad." This isn't the time to spring new lovers on him. "A friend made me a table. It's in the basement."

"How about chairs?" Ah, my good father. He could have said, friend? What friend?

Marge, my landlady, has all kinds of junky stuff in the basement. "Jorge and I'll bring up what we need. You'd strain your back, Dad." Shot knees, bad back: daily pain but nothing fatal. Not like Carmine.

"Jorge? Is that the new boyfriend?"

Shocking him makes me feel good. It would serve him right if Jorge were my new boyfriend. But Jorge is Marge's other roomer. He gives Marge Spanish lessons, and does the heavy cleaning and the yard work. Jorge has family in El Salvador he's hoping to bring up. I haven't met Marge's husband yet. He works on an offshore oil rig in some emirate with a funny name.

"No, Dad." I explain about Jorge.

"El Salvador!" he repeats. "That means 'the Savior.'" He passes on the information with a kind of awe. It makes Jorge's homeland, which he's shown me pretty pictures of, seem messy and exotic, at the very rim of human comprehension.

After Dad leaves, I call Cindi, who lives fifteen minutes away on Upper Mountainside Road. She's eleven months younger and almost a natural blond, but we're close. Brent wasn't easy for me to take, not at first. He owns a discount camera and electronics store on Fifty-fourth in Manhattan. Cindi met him through Club Med. They sat on a gorgeous Caribbean beach and talked of hogs. His father is an Amish farmer in Kalona, Iowa. Brent, in spite of the obvious hairpiece and the gold chain, is a rebel. He was born Schwartzendruber, but changed his name to Schwartz. Now no one believes the Brent, either. They call him Bernie on the street and it makes everyone more comfortable. His father's never taken their buggy out of the county.

The first time Vic asked me out, he talked of feminism and holism and macrobiotics. Then he opened up on cinema and literature, and I was very impressed, as who wouldn't be? Ro, my current lover, is very different. He picked me up in an uptown singles bar that I and sometimes Cindi go to. He bought me a Cinzano and touched my breast in the dark. He was direct, and at the same time weirdly courtly. I took him home though usually I don't, at first. I learned in bed that night that the tall brown drink with the lemon twist he'd been drinking was Tab.

I went back on the singles circuit even though the break with Vic should have made me cautious. Cindi thinks Vic's a romantic. I've told her how it ended. One Sunday morning in March he kissed me awake as usual. He'd brought in the *Times* from the porch and was reading it. I made us some cinnamon rose tea. We had a ritual, starting with the real estate pages, passing remarks on the latest tacky towers. Not for us, we'd say, the view is terrible! No room for the servants, things like that. And our imaginary children's imaginary nanny. "Hi, gorgeous," I said. He is gorgeous, not strong, but showy. He said, "I'm leaving, babe. New Jersey doesn't do it for me anymore." I said, "Okay, so where're we going?" I had an awful job at the time, taking orders for MCI. Vic said, "I didn't say we, babe." So I asked, "You mean it's over? Just like that?" And he said, "Isn't that the best way? No fuss, no hang-ups." Then I got a little whiny. "But *why*?" I wanted to know. But he was macrobiotic in lots of things, including relationships. Yin and yang, hot and sour, green and yellow. "You know, Rindy, there are *places*. You don't fall off the earth when you leave Jersey, you know. Places you see pictures of and read about. Different weathers, different trees, different everything. Places that get the Cubs on cable instead of the Mets." He was into that. For all the sophisticated things he liked to talk about, he was a very local boy. "Vic," I pleaded, "you're crazy. You need help." "I need help because I want to get out of Jersey? You gotta be kidding!" He stood up and for a moment I thought he would do something crazy, like destroy something, or hurt me. "Don't ever call me crazy, got that? And give me the keys to the van."

He took the van. Danny had sold it to me when the Marines sent him overseas. I'd have given it to him anyway, even if he hadn't asked.

"Cindi, I need a turkey roaster," I tell my sister on the phone.

"I'll be right over," she says. "The brat's driving me crazy."

"Isn't Franny's visit working out?"

"I could kill her. I think up ways. How does that sound?"

"Why not send her home?" I'm joking. Franny is Brent's twelve-year-old and he's shelled out a lot of dough to lawyers in New Jersey and Florida to work out visitation rights.

"Poor Brent. He feels so *divided*," Cindi says. "He shouldn't have to take sides."

I want her to ask who my date is for this afternoon, but she doesn't. It's important to me that she like Ro, that Mom and Dad more than tolerate him.

All over the country, I tell myself, women are towing new lovers home to meet their families. Vic is simmering cranberries in somebody's kitchen and explaining yin and yang. I check out the stuffing recipe. The gravy calls for cream and freshly grated nutmeg. Ro brought me six whole nutmegs in a Ziplock bag from his friend, a Pakistani, who runs a spice store in SoHo. The nuts look hard and ugly. I take one out of the bag and sniff it. The aroma's so exotic my head swims. On an impulse I call Ro.

The phone rings and rings. He doesn't have his own place yet. He has to crash with friends. He's been in the States three months, maybe less. I let it ring fifteen, sixteen, seventeen times.

Finally someone answers. "Yes?" The voice is guarded, the accent obviously foreign even though all I'm hearing is a one-syllable word. Ro has fled here from Kabul. He wants to take classes at NJIT and become an electrical engineer. He says he's lucky his father got him out. A friend of Ro's father, a man called Mumtaz, runs a fried chicken restaurant in Brooklyn in a neighborhood Ro calls "Little Kabul," though probably no one else has ever noticed. Mr. Mumtaz puts the legal immigrants to work as waiters out front. The illegals hide in a backroom as pluckers and gutters.

"Ro? I miss you. We're eating at three, remember?"

"Who is speaking, please?"

So I fell for the accent, but it isn't a malicious error. I *can* tell one Afghan tribe from another now, even by looking at them or by their names. I can make out some Pashto words. "Tell Ro it's Rindy. Please? I'm a friend. He wanted me to call this number."

"Not knowing any Ro."

"Hey, wait. Tell him it's Rindy deMarco."

The guy hangs up on me.

I'm crumbling cornbread into a bowl for the stuffing when Cindi honks half of "King Cotton" from the parking apron in the back. Brent bought her the BMW on the gray market and saved a bundle—once discount, always discount—then spent three hundred dollars to put in a horn that beeps a Sousa march. I wave a potato masher at her from the back window. She doesn't get out of the car. Instead she points to the pan in the back seat. I come down, wiping my hands on a dish towel.

"I should stay and help." Cindi sounds ready to cry. But I don't want her with me when Ro calls back.

"You're doing too much already, kiddo." My voice at least sounds comforting. "You promised one veg and the salad."

"I ought to come up and help. That or get drunk." She shifts the stick. When Brent bought her the car, the dealer threw in driving gloves to match the upholstery.

"Get Franny to shred the greens," I call as Cindi backs up the car. "Get her involved."

The phone is ringing in my apartment. I can hear it ring from the second-floor landing.

"Ro?"

"You're taking a chance, my treasure. It could have been any other admirer, then where would you be?"

"I don't have any other admirers." Ro is not a conventionally jealous man, not like the types I have known. He's totally unlike any man I have ever known. He wants men to come on to me. Lately when we go to a bar he makes me sit far enough from him so some poor lonely guy thinks I'm looking for action. Ro likes to swagger out of a dark booth as soon as someone buys me a drink. I go along. He comes from a macho culture.

"How else will I know you are as beautiful as I think you are? I would not want an unprized woman," he says. He is asking me for time, I know. In a few more months he'll know I'm something of a catch in my culture, or at least I've never had trouble finding boys. Even Brent Schwartzendruber has begged me to see him alone.

"I'm going to be a little late," Ro says. "I told you about my cousin, Abdul, no?"

Ro has three or four cousins that I know of in Manhattan. They're all named Abdul something. When I think of Abdul, I think of a giant black man with goggles on, running down a court. Abdul is the teenage cousin whom immigration officials nabbed as he was gutting chickens in Mumtaz's backroom.

Abdul doesn't have the right papers to live and work in this country, and now he's been locked up in a detention center on Varick Street. Ro's afraid Abdul will be deported back to Afghanistan. If that happens, he'll be tortured.

"I have to visit him before I take the DeCamp bus. He's talking nonsense. He's talking of starting a hunger fast."

"A hunger strike! God!" When I'm with Ro I feel I am looking at America through the wrong end of a telescope. He makes it sound like a police state, with sudden raids, papers, detention centers, deportations, and torture and death waiting in the wings. I'm not a political person. Last fall I wore the Ferraro button because she's a woman and Italian.

"Rindy, all night I've been up and awake. All night I think of your splendid breasts. Like clusters of grapes, I think. I am stroking and fondling your grapes this very minute. My talk gets you excited?"

I tell him to test me, please get here before three. I remind him he can't buy his ticket on the bus.

"We got here too early, didn't we?" Dad stands just outside the door to my apartment, looking embarrassed. He's in his best dark suit, the one he wears every Thanksgiving and Christmas. This year he can't do up the top button of his jacket.

"Don't be so formal, Dad." I give him a showy hug and pull him indoors so Mom can come in.

"As if your papa ever listens to me!" Mom laughs. But she sits primly on the sofa bed in her velvet cloak, with her tote bag and evening purse on her lap. Before Dad started courting her, she worked as a seamstress. Dad rescued her from a sweatshop. He married down, she married well. That's the family story.

"She told me to rush."

Mom isn't in a mood to squabble. I think she's reached the point of knowing she won't have him forever. There was Carmine, at death's door just a month ago. Anything could happen to Dad. She says, "Renata, look what I made! Crostolis." She lifts a cake tin out of her tote bag. The pan still feels warm. And for dessert, I know, there'll be a jar of super-thick, super-rich Death by Chocolate.

The story about Grandma deMarco, Dad's mama, is that every Thanksgiving she served two full dinners, one American with the roast turkey, candied yams, pumpkin pie, the works, and another with Grandpa's favorite pastas.

Dad relaxes. He appoints himself bartender. "Don't you have more ice cubes, sweetheart?"

I tell him it's good Glenlivet. He shouldn't ruin it with ice, just a touch of water if he must. Dad pours sherry in Vic's pottery espresso cups for his women. Vic made them himself, and I used to think they were perfect blue jewels. Now I see they're lumpy, uneven in color.

"Go change into something pretty before Carla and Brent come." Mom believes in dressing up. Beaded dresses lift her spirits. She's wearing a beaded green dress today.

I take the sherry and vanish behind a four-panel screen, the kind long-legged showgirls change behind in black and white movies while their moustached lovers keep talking. My head barely shows above the screen's top, since I'm no long-legged showgirl. My best points, as Ro has said, are my clusters of grapes. Vic found the screen at a country auction in the Adirondacks. It had filled the van. Now I use the panels as a bulletin board and I'm worried Dad'll spot the notice for the next meeting of Amnesty International, which will bother him. He will think the two words stand for draft dodger and communist. I was going to drop my membership, a legacy of Vic, when Ro saw it and approved. Dad goes to the Sons of Italy Anti-Defamation dinners. He met Frank Sinatra at one. He voted for Reagan last time because the Democrats ran an Italian woman.

Instead of a thirties lover, it's my moustached papa talking to me from the other side of the screen. "So where's this dining table?"

"Ro's got the parts in the basement. He'll bring it up, Dad."

I hear them whispering. "Bo? Now she's messing with a Southerner?" and "Shh, it's her business."

I'm just smoothing on my pantyhose when Mom screams for the cops. Dad shouts too, at Mom for her to shut up. It's my fault, I should have warned Ro not to use his key this afternoon.

I peek over the screen's top and see my lover the way my parents see him. He's a slight, pretty man with hazel eyes and a tufty moustache, so whom can he intimidate? I've seen Jews and Greeks, not to mention Sons of Italy, darker-skinned than Ro. Poor Ro resorts to his Kabuli prep-school manners.

"How do you do, Madam! Sir! My name is Roashan."

Dad moves closer to Ro but doesn't hold out his hand. I can almost read his mind: *he speaks.* "Come again?" he says, baffled.

I cringe as he spells his name. My parents are so parochial. With each letter he does a graceful dip and bow. "Try it syllable by syllable, sir. Then it is not so hard."

Mom stares past him at me. The screen doesn't hide me because I've strayed too far in to watch the farce. "Renata, you're wearing only your camisole."

I pull my crew neck over my head, then kiss him. I make the kiss really sexy so they'll know I've slept with this man. Many times. And if he asks me, I will marry him. I had not known that till now. I think my mother guesses.

He's brought flowers: four long-stemmed, stylish purple blossoms in a florist's paper cone. "For you, madam." He glides over the dirty broadloom to Mom who fills up more than half the sofa bed. "This is my first Thanksgiving dinner, for which I have much to give thanks, no?"

"He was born in Afghanistan," I explain. But Dad gets continents wrong. He says, "We saw your famine camps on TV. Well, you won't starve this afternoon."

"They smell good," Mom says. "Thank you very much but you shouldn't spend a fortune."

"No, no, madam. What you smell good is my cologne. Flowers in New York have no fragrance."

"His father had a garden estate outside Kabul." I don't want

Mom to think he's putting down American flowers, though in fact he is. Along with American fruits, meats, and vegetables. "The Russians bulldozed it," I add.

Dad doesn't want to talk politics. He senses, looking at Ro, this is not the face of Ethiopian starvation. "Well, what'll it be, Roy? Scotch and soda?" I wince. It's not going well.

"Thank you but no. I do not imbibe alcoholic spirits, though I have no objection for you, sir." My lover goes to the fridge and reaches down. He knows just where to find his Tab. My father is quietly livid, staring down at his drink.

In my father's world, grown men bowl in leagues and drink the best whiskey they can afford. Dad whistles "My Way." He must be under stress. That's his usual self-therapy: how would Francis Albert handle this?

"Muslims have taboos, Dad." Cindi didn't marry a Catholic, so he has no right to be upset about Ro, about us.

"Jews," Dad mutters. "So do Jews." He knows because catty-corner from Vitelli's is a kosher butcher. This isn't the time to parade new words before him, like *halal*, the Muslim kosher. An Italian-American man should be able to live sixty-five years never having heard the word, I can go along with that. Ro, fortunately, is cosmopolitan. Outside of pork and booze, he eats anything else I fix.

Brent and Cindi take forever to come. But finally we hear his MG squeal in the driveway. Ro glides to the front window; he seems to blend with the ficus tree and hanging ferns. Dad and I wait by the door.

"Party time!" Brent shouts as he maneuvers Cindi and Franny ahead of him up three flights of stairs. He looks very much the head of the family, a rich man steeply in debt to keep up appearances, to compete, to head off middle age. He's at that age—and Cindi's nowhere near that age—when people notice the difference and quietly judge it. I know these things from Cindi—I'd never guess it from looking at Brent. If he feels divided, as Cindi says he does, it doesn't show. Misery, anxiety, whatever, show on Cindi though; they bring her cheekbones out. When I'm depressed, my hair looks rough, my skin breaks out. Right now, I'm lustrous.

Brent does a lot of whooping and hugging at the door. He even hugs Dad who looks grave and funereal like an old-world Italian gentleman because of his outdated, pinched dark suit. Cindi makes straight for the fridge with her casserole of squash and browned marshmallow. Franny just stands in the middle of the room holding two biggish Baggies of salad greens and vinaigrette in an old Dijon mustard jar. Brent actually bought the mustard in Dijon, a story that Ro is bound to hear and not appreciate. Vic was mean enough last year to tell him that he could have gotten it for more or less the same price at the Italian specialty foods store down on Watchung Plaza. Franny doesn't seem to have her own winter clothes. She's wearing Cindi's car coat over a Dolphins sweatshirt. Her mother moved down to Florida the very day the divorce became final. She's got a Walkman tucked into the pocket of her cords.

"You could have trusted me to make the salad dressing at least," I scold my sister.

Franny gives up the Baggies and the jar of dressing to me. She scrutinizes us—Mom, Dad, me and Ro, especially Ro, as though she can detect something strange about him—but doesn't take off her earphones. A smirk starts twitching her tanned, feral features. I see what she is seeing. Asian men carry their bodies differently, even these famed warriors from the Khyber Pass. Ro doesn't stand like Brent or Dad. His hands hang kind of stiffly from the shoulder joints, and when he moves, his palms are tucked tight against his thighs, his stomach sticks out like a slightly pregnant woman's. Each culture establishes its own manly posture, different ways of claiming space. Ro, hiding among my plants, holds himself in a way that seems both too effeminate and too macho. I hate Franny for what she's doing to me. I am twenty-seven years old, I should be more mature. But I see now how wrong Ro's clothes are. He shows too much white collar and cuff. His shirt and his wool-blend flare-leg pants were made to measure in Kabul. The jacket comes from a discount store on Canal Street, part of a discontinued line of two-trousered suits. I ought to know, I took him there. I want to shake Franny or smash the earphones.

Cindi catches my exasperated look. "Don't pay any attention to her. She's unsociable this weekend. We can't compete with the Depeche Mode."

I intend to compete.

Franny, her eyes very green and very hostile, turns on Brent. "How come she never gets it right, Dad?"

Brent hi-fives his daughter, which embarrasses her more than anyone else in the room. "It's a Howard Jones, hon," Brent tells Cindi.

Franny, close to tears, runs to the front window where Ro's been hanging back. She has an ungainly walk for a child whose support payments specify weekly ballet lessons. She bores in on Ro's hidey hole like Russian artillery. Ro moves back to the perimeter of family intimacy. I have no way of helping yet. I have to set out the dips and Tostitos. Brent and Dad are talking sports, Mom and Cindi are watching the turkey. Dad's going on about the Knicks. He's in despair, so early in the season. He's on his second Scotch. I see Brent try. "What do you think, Roy?" He's doing his best to get my lover involved. "Maybe we'll get lucky, huh? We can always hope for a top draft pick. End up with Patrick Ewing!" Dad brightens. "That guy'll change the game. Just wait and see. He'll fill the lane better than Russell." Brent gets angry, since for some strange Amish reason he's a Celtics fan. So was Vic. "Bird'll make a monkey out of him." He looks to Ro for support.

Ro nods. Even his headshake is foreign. "You are undoubtedly correct, Brent," he says. "I am deferring to your judgment because currently I have not familiarized myself with these practices."

Ro loves squash, but none of my relatives have ever picked up a racket. I want to tell Brent that Ro's skied in St. Moritz, lost a thousand dollars in a casino in Beirut, knows where to buy Havana cigars without getting hijacked. He's sophisticated, he could make monkeys out of us all, but they think he's a retard.

Brent drinks three Scotches to Dad's two; then all three men go down to the basement. Ro and Brent do the carrying, negotiating sharp turns in the stairwell. Dad supervises. There are two trestles and a wide, splintery plywood top. "Try not to take the wall down!" Dad yells.

When they make it back in, the men take off their jackets to assemble the table. Brent's wearing a red lamb's wool turtleneck under his camel hair blazer. Ro unfastens his cuff links—they are 24-karat gold and his father's told him to sell them if funds run low—and pushes up his very white shirt sleeves. There are scars on both arms, scars that bubble against his dark skin, scars like lightning flashes under his thick black hair. Scar tissue on Ro is the color of freshwater pearls. I want to kiss it.

Cindi checks the turkey one more time. "You guys better hurry. We'll be ready to eat in fifteen minutes."

Ro, the future engineer, adjusts the trestles. He's at his best now. He's become quite chatty. From under the plywood top, he's holding forth on the Soviet menace in Kabul. Brent may actually have an idea where Afghanistan is, in a general way, but Dad is lost. He's talking of being arrested for handing out pro-American pamphlets on his campus. Dad stiffens at "arrest" and blanks out the rest. He talks of this "so-called leader," this "criminal" named Babrak Karmal and I hear other buzz-words like Kandahār and Pamir, words that might have been Polish to me a month ago, and I can see even Brent is slightly embarrassed. It's his first exposure to Third World passion. He thought only Americans had informed political opinion—other people staged coups out of spite and misery. It's an unwelcome revelation to him that a reasonably educated and rational man like Ro would die for things that he, Brent, has never heard of and would rather laugh about. Ro was tortured in jail. Franny has taken off her earphones. Electrodes, canes, freezing tanks. He leaves nothing out. Something's gotten into Ro.

Dad looks sick. The meaning of Thanksgiving should not be so explicit. But Ro's in a daze. He goes on about how—*inshallah*—his father, once a rich landlord, had stashed away enough to bribe a guard, sneak him out of this cell and hide him for four months in a tunnel dug under a servant's adobe hut until a forged American visa could be bought. Franny's eyes are wide, Dad joins Mom on the sofa bed, shaking his head. Jail, bribes, forged, what is this? I can read his mind. "For six days I must orbit one international airport to another," Ro is saying. "The main trick is having a valid ticket, that way the airline has to carry you, even if the country won't take you in. Colombo, Seoul, Bombay, Geneva, Frankfurt, I know too too well the transit lounges of many airports. We travel the world with our gym bags and prayer rugs, unrolling them in the transit lounges. The better airports have special rooms."

Brent tries to ease Dad's pain. "Say, buddy," he jokes, "you wouldn't be ripping us off, would you?"

Ro snakes his slender body from under the makeshift table. He hasn't been watching the effect of his monologue. "I am a working man," he says stiffly. I have seen his special permit. He's one of the lucky ones, though it might not last. He's saving for NJIT. Meantime he's gutting chickens to pay for room and board in Little Kabul. He describes the gutting process. His face is transformed as he sticks his fist into imaginary roasters and grabs for gizzards, pulls out the squishy stuff. He takes an Afghan dagger out of the pocket of his pants. You'd never guess, he looks like such a victim. "This," he says, eyes glinting. "This is all I need."

"Cool," Franny says.

"Time to eat," Mom shouts. "I made the gravy with the nutmeg as you said, Renata."

73

I lead Dad to the head of the table. "Everyone else sit where you want to."

Franny picks out the chair next to Ro before I can put Cindi there. I want Cindi to know him, I want her as an ally.

Dad tests the blade of the carving knife. Mom put the knife where Dad always sits when she set the table. He takes his thumb off the blade and pushes the switch. "That noise makes me feel good."

But I carry in the platter with the turkey and place it in front of Ro. "I want you to carve," I say.

He brings out his dagger all over again. Franny is practically licking his fingers. "You mean this is a professional job?"

We stare fascinated as my lover slashes and slices, swiftly, confidently, at the huge, browned, juicy breast. The dagger scoops out flesh.

Now I am the one in a daze. I am seeing Ro's naked body as though for the first time, his nicked, scarred, burned body. In his body, the blemishes seem embedded, more beautiful, like wood. I am seeing character made manifest. I am seeing Brent and Dad for the first time, too. They have their little scars, things they're proud of, football injuries and bowling elbows they brag about. Our scars are so innocent; they are invisible and come to us from rough-housing gone too far. Ro hates to talk about his scars. If I trace the puckered tissue on his left thigh and ask "How, Ro?" he becomes shy, dismissive: a pack of dogs attacked him when he was a boy. The skin on his back is speckled and lumpy from burns, but when I ask he laughs. A crazy villager whacked him with a burning stick for cheekiness, he explains. He's ashamed that he comes from a culture of pain.

The turkey is reduced to a drying, whitened skeleton. On our plates, the slices are symmetrical, elegant. I realize all in a rush how much I love this man with his blemished, tortured body. I will give him citizenship if he asks. Vic was beautiful, but Vic was self-sufficient. Ro's my chance to heal the world.

I shall teach him how to walk like an American, how to dress like Brent but better, how to fill up a room as Dad does instead of melting and blending but sticking out in the Afghan way. In spite of the funny way he holds himself and the funny way he moves his head from side to side when he wants to say yes, Ro is Clint Eastwood, scarred hero and survivor. Dad and Brent are children. I realize Ro's the only circumcised man I've slept with.

Mom asks, "Why are you grinning like that, Renata?"

FIGHTING
FOR
THE
REBOUND

I'M in bed watching the Vanilla Gorilla stick it to the Abilene Christians on some really obscure cable channel when Blanquita comes through the door wearing lavender sweats, and over them a frilly see-through apron. It's a November Thursday, a chilly fifty-three, but she's hibachiing butterfly lamb on the balcony.

"Face it, Griff," Blanquita says, wielding the barbecue fork the way empresses wield scepters.

"Face what?"

"That's what I mean," she says. "You're so insensitive, it's awesome."

"Nobody says awesome anymore," I tease. Blanquita speaks six languages, her best being Tagalog, Spanish, and American.

"Why not?" she says. Back in Manila, she took a crash course in making nice to Americans, before her father sent her over. In her family they called her Baby. "Bite him, Marcos," she orders her cat. "Spit on him." But Marcos chooses to stay behind the harpsichord and leggy ficus. Marcos knows I am not a cat person; he's known me to sneak in a kick. He takes out his hostilities on the ficus. What he does is chew up a pale, new leaf. I get my greenery for free because the office I work in throws out all browning, scraggly plants and trees. I have an arboretum of rejects.

"Let's start this conversation over," I plead. I'm tentative at the start of relationships, but this time I'm not throwing it away.

"Let's," she says.

"You're beautiful," I say.

"Do you mean that?"

I hate it when she goes intense on me. She starts to lift off the Press-On Nails from her thumbs. Her own nails are roundish and ridged, which might be her only imperfection.

"Blanquita the Beautiful." I shoot it through with melody. If I were a songwriter I'd write her a million lyrics. About frangipani blooms and crescent moons. But what I am is a low-level money manager, a solid, decent guy in white shirt and maroon tie and thinning, sandy hair over which hangs the sword of Damocles. The Dow Jones crowds my chest like an implant. I unlist my telephone every six weeks, and still they find me, the widows and orthodontists into the money-market. I feel the sword's point every minute. Get me in futures! In Globals, in Aggressive Growth, in bonds! I try to tell them, for every loser there's a winner, somewhere. Someone's always profiting, just give me time and I'll find it, I'll lock you in it.

Blanquita scoops Marcos off the broadloom and holds him on her hip as she might a baby. "I should never have left Manila," she says. She does some very heavy, very effective sighing. "Pappy was right. The East is East and the West is West and never the twain shall meet."

I get these nuggets from Kipling at least once a week. "But, baby," I object, "you did leave. Atlanta is halfway around the world from the Philippines."

"Poor Pappy," Blanquita moons. "Poor Joker."

She doesn't give me much on her family other than that Pappy—Joker Rosario—a one-time big-shot publisher tight with the Marcos crew, is stuck in California stocking shelves in a liquor store. Living like a peon, serving winos in some hotbox *barrio*. Mother runs a beauty shop out of her kitchen in West Hartford, Connecticut. His politics, and those of his daughter, are—to understate it—vile. She'd gotten to America long before his fall, when he still had loot and power and loved to spread it around. She likes to act as though real life began for her at JFK when she got past the customs and immigration on the seventeenth of October, 1980. That's fine with me. The less I know about growing up in Manila, rich or any other way, the less foreign she feels. Dear old redneck Atlanta is a thing of the past, no need to feel foreign here. Just wheel your shopping cart through aisles of bok choy and twenty kinds of Jamaican spices at the Farmers' Market, and you'll see that the US of A is still a pioneer country.

She relaxes, and Marcos leaps off the sexy, shallow shelf of her left hip. "You're a racist, patronizing jerk if you think I'm beautiful. I'm just different, that's all."

"Different from whom?"

"All your others."

It's in her interest, somehow, to imagine me as Buckhead's primo swinger, maybe because—I can't be sure—she needs the buzz of perpetual jealousy. She needs to feel herself a temp. For all the rotten things she says about the Philippines, or the mistiness she reserves for the Stars and Stripes, she's kept her old citizenship.

"Baby, Baby, don't do this to me. Please?"

I crank up the Kraftmatic. My knees, drawn up and tense, push against my forehead. Okay, so maybe what I meant was that she isn't a looker in the blondhair-smalltits-greatlegs way that Wendi was. Or Emilou, for that matter. But beautiful is how she makes me feel. Wendi was slow-growth. Emilou was strictly Chapter Eleven.

I can't tell her that. I can't tell her I've been trading on rumor, selling on news, for years. Your smart pinstriper aims for the short-term profit. My track record for pickin 'em is just a little better than blindfold darts. It's as hard to lose big these days as it is to make a killing. I understand those inside traders—it's not the money, it's the rush. I'm hanging in for the balance of the quarter.

But.

If there's a shot, I'll take it.

Meantime, the barbecue fork in Blanquita's hand describes circles of such inner distress that I have to take my eyes off the slaughter of the Abilene Christians.

"You don't love me, Griff."

It's hard to know where she learns her lines. They're all so tragically sincere. Maybe they go back to the instant-marriage emporiums in Manila. Or the magazines she reads. Or a series of married, misunderstood men that she must have introduced to emotional chaos. Her tastes in everything are, invariably, unspeakable. She rests a kneecap on the twisted Kraftmatic and weeps. Even her kneecaps . . . well, even the kneecaps get my attention. It's not fair. Behind her, the Vanilla Gorilla is going man-to-man. Marcos is about to strangle himself with orange wool he's pawed out of a dusty wicker yarn basket. Wendi was a knitter. Love flees, but we're stuck with love's debris.

"I'm not saying you don't *like* me, Griff. I'm saying you don't love me, okay?"

Why do I think she's said it all before? Why do I hear "sailor" instead of my name? "Don't spoil what we have." I am begging.

She believes me. Her face goes radiant. "What do we have, Griff?" Then she backs away from my hug. She believes me not.

All I get to squeeze are hands adorned with the glamor-length Press-On Nails. She could make a fortune as a hands model if she wanted to. That skin of hers is an evolutionary leap. Holding hands on the bed, we listen for a bit to the lamb spit fat. Anyone can suffer a cold shooting spell. I'm thirty-three and a vet of Club Med vacations; I can still ballhandle, but one-on-one is a younger man's game.

"All right, we'll drop the subject," Blanquita says. "I can be a good sport."

"That's my girl," I say. But I can tell from the angle of her chin and the new stiffness of her posture that she's turning prim and well-brought-up on me. Then she lobs devastation. "I won't be seeing you this weekend."

"It's *ciao* because I haven't bought you a ring?"

"No," she says, haughtily. "The Chief's asked me out, that's why. We're going up to his cabin."

I don't believe her. She's not the Chief's type. She wants to goad me into confessing that I love her.

"You're a fast little worker." The Chief, a jowly fifty-five, is rumored to enjoy exotic tastes. But, Christ, there's a difference between exotic and *foreign*, isn't there? Exotic means you know how to use your foreignness, or you make yourself a little foreign in order to appear exotic. Real foreign is a little scary, believe me. The fact is, the Chief brought Blanquita and me together in his office. That was nearly six months ago. I was there to prep him, and she was hustled in, tools of the trade stuffed into a Lancôme tote sack, to make him look good on TV. Blanquita's a makeup artist on the way up and up, and Atlanta is Executives City, where every Chief wants to look terrific before he throws himself to the corporate lions. I watched her operate. She pumped him up a dozen ways. And I just sat there, stunned. The Chief still had moves.

"You sound jealous, Griff." She turns her wicked, bottom-less blacks on me and I feel myself squirm.

"Go up to the cabin if you want to. I don't do jealousy, hon."

She starts trapping on defense herself now. "You don't do jealousy! Well, you don't have the right to be jealous! You don't have any rights, period! You can't change the ground rules!"

Maybe Wendi wasn't all that certifiable a disaster. Come to think of it, Wendi had her moments. She could be a warm, nurturing person. We talked, we did things together. The summer we were breaking up, I built her kid a treehouse, which might be the only unselfish good I've accomplished in my life. Blanquita's a Third World aristocrat, a hothouse orchid you worship but don't dare touch. I wouldn't dare ask her to help me knock together a bookcase or scrub the grout around the bathroom tiles. But Wendi, alas, never made me feel this special, this loved.

"I'm serious, Griff." She closes her eyes and rams her fists in eyelids that are as delicately mauve as her sweatshirt. "You keep me in limbo. I need to know where we stand."

"I don't want you to go," I say. I'm not myself. I'm a romantic in red suspenders.

"What do you want me to do?"

"Whatever you want to do, hon."

Her body sags inside her oversized sweatshirt. She gets off the mattress, strokes Marcos with the toes of her Reeboks, checks a shredded ficus leaf, tosses the skein of orange wool from the balcony down to the parking lot.

"Hullo," I say. "Hey, Baby." I really want to reach her. "Hey, watch him!" Wendi was a big basketball fan, a refugee from Hoosierland, and she was the first and so far the only woman I've known who could sit through a Braves or Falcons game. If I could get Miss Bataan to watch the Gorilla stuff it, we'd be okay, but she doesn't even pretend to watch.

"I'm going to make myself a cup of tea," she says.

We say nothing while she brews herself a pot of cherry almond. Then she sits on my bed and drinks a slow cup, fiddling with the remote control and putting to flight all ten sweaty goons. F. Lee Bailey comes on and talks up the Bhopal tragedy. I can't believe it's been a year. I must have been seeing Emilou on the side when it happened. Yes, in fact Emilou cried, and Wendi had made a fuss about the mascara on my sixty-buck shirt. An auditorium packed with Herbalifers comes on the screen. The Herbalifers are very upbeat and very free enterprise. They perk her up.

"We don't need that," I plead.

"You don't know what you need," she snaps. "You're so narcissistic you don't need anyone. You don't know how to love."

Sailor, I think. It thrills me.

"That's not fair."

But Blanquita the Beautiful races on to bigger issues. "Not just you, Griff," she scolds in that eerily well-bred, Asian convent-schooled voice. "You're all emotional cripples. All you Americans. You just worry about your own measly little relationships. You don't care how much you hurt the world."

In changing gears, she's right up there with Mario Andretti. I envy her her freedom, her Green Card politics. It's love, not justice, that powers her. Emilou and Wendi would have died if I caught them in an inconsistency.

She jabs at more buttons on the remote control doodad. Herbalifers scuttle into permanent blackness, and a Soweto funeral procession comes on. Big guys in black boots come at pallbearers with whips and clubs. Blanquita lays her teacup on the top sheet. These are serious designer sheets, debris from my months with Emilou. When Joker Rosario went to South Africa back in the long, long ago, he was treated very, very white. He wrote pleasant things about South Africa in his paper. Yesterday's statesman is today's purveyor of Muscatel. South Africa is making her morose, and I dare not ask why. I suddenly remember that the neighborhood dry cleaner doesn't know how to take tea stains off but does a good job with Kahlúa. Blanquita flashes the black inscrutables one more time and says, "I can't stand it anymore, Griff. It's got to stop."

South Africa? I wonder, but dare not hope. I carefully remove her teacup and take hold of her fingertips, which are still warm from holding the cup, and pull them up to my beard. "We have each other," I say.

"Do we?"

It's time to take charge, to force the good times to roll. Some nations were built to take charge. It's okay for a nation of pioneers to bully the rest of the world as long as the cause is just. My heart is pure, my head is clear. I retrieve the doodad from Blanquita's perfect hand. I want to show her the funtimes of TV-land. I slice through a Mexican variety show on SIN. Any time of the day or night, those Mexicans are in tuxedos.

All those blow-dried Mexican emcees in soccer stadiums, look-ing like Ricardo Montalbans who never made it.

I know she's a secret fan.

On cue, my trusty nineteen-incher serves up the right stuff. It's National Cheerleading Contest time. A squad in skimpy skirts, Oceanside High's cutest, synchronizes cartwheels and handstands, and starts to dust the competition. I feel godly powers surge through my body as Blanquita relaxes. Soon she relaxes enough to laugh.

"Did you ever try out as a cheerleader?" I ask. I can sense the imminence of terrific times.

Blanquita the Beautiful watches the kids on the screen with gratifying intensity. Then she thrusts a hesitant leg in the air. It's the fault of the French maid's apron that she's wearing over her baggy sweats; my saucy exotic's turned a schoolgirl routine into something alien and absurd. Oh, Blanquita, not so fast!

"I'm too good for you, Griff," she pants, twirling an invisible baton and high-stepping across the condo's wall-to-wall. "Pappy would call you illiterate scum."

"And so I am. But Joker's selling rotgut through a retractable grate and Mama's perming Koreans in her living room. Ferdie and Imelda they're not." If People Power hadn't cut them down, if Joker's own reporters hadn't locked him out, Blanquita was promised a place in the Miss Universe contest. That's why she kept her citizenship.

"That's needlessly cruel."

"Baby, you've got to stop living in the past."

"Okay." She stops the twirling and marching. She turns the TV off without the doodad though I've begged her not to many times. Without the light from the screen, the condo room seems as dull and impersonal as a room in a Holiday Inn.

Without Blanquita I'd be just another Joe Blow Buckhead yuppie in his Reeboks. It's she who brings me to bed each night and wakes me up each morning, big as a house and hard as a sidewalk.

"Okay," she goes again. "Who needs a crummy tropical past?"

We're out of the woods. I start to relax.

"Two cheers for cable sleaze." I shout. She plucks Marcos from his hidey hole behind the ficus and babies him. "I'm saying yes to the Chief, Griff. Hip, Hip!"

"What?"

"He says I make him look like a million dollars and make him feel like even more."

"Get it in writing. That's a low-rent come-on. He wouldn't dare try it on the office girls."

"Of course not."

She's not been getting my point.

"I have to get on with my life. And anyway, you said you weren't jealous so what's to hold me up?"

I check out her pulse rate with my lips. I'm not verbal. Maybe I don't love Blanquita. Because I don't know what love is. I'm not ready for one-on-one.

Baby Blanquita is too agitated to smell the charred lamb whooshing off the hibachi, so it's up to me, the narcissist, to rescue the rescue-worthy. The balcony that holds the smoking hibachi is eighteen floors up. Standing between the high gray sky and the pocket-sized pool, I feel omnipotent. Everything's in place.

While I poke the ruined meat with the barbecue fork, an uncommonly handsome blond woman in a ponytail and a cherry-red tracksuit comes out of the building's back door. She hurls a bashed pizza box, like a Frisbee, into the dumpster. Excess energy floats toward me, connecting us. She can't stand still. She tightens a shoelace. We're a community of toned, conditioned athletes. Use it or lose it. Hands pressed down on somebody's Firebird, she does warm-up routines. I've seen her run in the Lullwater Estate close by, but I've never felt connected enough to her to nod. I heave the meat from the rack to a platter. The woman's still hanging around in that hyper, fidgety way of hers. She's waiting. She's waiting for someone. When a man in a matching tracksuit jogs out the back door, I get depressed. She used to run alone.

Blanquita doesn't say anything about the state of our dinner. It's already stuffed away conveniently in the past. She's got the TV going again. The latest news, hot from Mexico City. "They had this news analyst chap on a minute ago," she says. "They were talking about Vitaly Yurchenko."

I put the butterfly lamb in the kitchen sink. "Why don't you watch about Vitaly Yurchenko on an American station?" I ask. Usually, that steams her. Mexican *is* American! she'll squeal. But instead she says, "He could have had it all if he'd stayed. What's so great about Moscow?"

"Sometimes you blow it for love. It can happen."

She runs to me, lavender arms going like wings. Her face—the skin so tight-pored that in the dark I feel I'm stroking petals—glows with new hope. "What are you saying, Griff? Are you saying what I think you're saying?"

I know what I would say if I weren't the solid corporate guy in maroon tie and dark suit. I buy and sell with other people's money and skim enough to just get by. It's worked so far.

"Griff?"

Sailor?

"Let's go for a run, Blanquita."

The woman of many men's dreams doesn't wrench herself free from my kissing hold. I don't deserve her.

"Just a short run. To clear our heads. Please?"

Before I met her I used to pump iron. I was pumping so hard I could feel a vein nearly pop in the back of my head. I was a candidate for a stroke. Self-love may be too much like self-hate, who knows? Blanquita got me running. We started out real easy, staying inside the Lullwater Estate like that woman in the red tracksuit. We ran the Peachtree 10K. We could run a marathon if we wanted to. Our weightless feet beat perfect time through city streets and wooded ravines. The daily run is the second best thing we do together, I like to think.

"All right," she says. She gives me one of her demure, convent smiles. "But what'll we do with dinner?"

I point at the shrivelled, carbonized thing in the stainless steel sink. "We could mail it to Africa."

"Biafra?" she asks.

"Baby, Baby . . . Ethiopia, Mozambique. Biafra was gone a long time ago," I tell her. She's very selective with her news. Emilou was a news hound, and I took to watching CNN for a solid winter.

Blanquita pins my condo key to her elasticized waistband and goes out the front door ahead of me. The lawyer from 1403 is waiting by the elevator. I am far enough behind Blanquita to catch the quickie gleam in his eyes before he resumes his cool Duke demeanor and holds the elevator for us. In your face, Blue Devil.

That night Blanquita whips up some green nutritive complexion cream in the Cuisinart. She slaps the green sludge on her face with a rubber spatula. Her face is unequivocally mournful. The sludge in the Cuisinart fills the condo with smells I remember from nature trails of my childhood. Woodsy growths. Mosses. Ferns. I tracked game as a kid; I fished creeks. Atlanta wasn't always this archipelago of developments.

"Better make tonight memorable," she advises. The mask is starting to stiffen, especially around the lips. She has full, pouty, brownish lips. "It's our last night."

How many times has she said that? I've never said it, never had to. The women of my life always got the idea in plenty of time, they made it a mutual-consent, too-bad and so-long kind of thing. Wendi was really looking for a stepfather to her kids. Emilou was looking for full-time business advice to manage her settlement.

"What's that supposed to mean?"

The lips make a whistling noise from inside the mask's cut-out. "Anyway," she says, "it wasn't all cherry bombs and rockets for me either. Just sparklers."

Sex, intimacy, love. I can't keep any of it straight anymore.

"You're not going to the Chief's cabin in the north woods, period. He's Jack the Ripper."

"You think I can't handle the situation, right? You think I'm just a dumb, naive foreigner you have to protect, right?"

"Yeah."

Then she leaps on me, green face, glamor-length nails, Dior robe and all. I don't know about Baby, but for me those rockets explode.

All day Sunday it rains. The raindrops are of the big, splashy variety, complete with whiffs of wild winds and churned seas. Our winter is starting. I don't do much; I stay in, play Bach on the earphones and vacuum the broadloom. Marcos seems here to stay because I can't bring myself to call the ASPCA.

When the hour for the daily run rolls around, I start out as usual in the doctors' wing of the VA Hospital parking lot, pick my way around Mazdas, Audis, Volvos—they don't have too many station wagons in this neighborhood—keep pace with fit groups in running shoes for as long as it feels good, then shoot ahead, past the serious runners who don't look back when they hear you coming, past the dogs with Frisbees in their jaws, past the pros who scorn designer tracksuits and the Emory runners with fraternity gizmos on their shirts, pick up more speed until the Reeboks sheathe feet as light as cotton. Then it's time to race. Really race. After Emilou and just before Baby I did wind sprints for a spring at the Atlanta Track Club, ran the three-minute half, ran four of them. I can let it out.

Today in the rain and the changing weather, colder tomorrow, I run longer, pushing harder, than any afternoon in my life. Running is here to stay, even if Baby is gone.

Today I run until a vein in the back of my head feels ready to pop. The stopgap remedy is Fiorinal, and so I pop one while I slump in the shower. It feels so good, the exhaustion, the pile of heavy, cold, sweaty clothes, the whole paraphernalia of deliberate self-depletion. At the track club they had a sign from William Butler Yeats: Torture Body to Pleasure Soul. I believe it.

What to do now? The rain is over, the Falcons are dying on the tube, the sun is staging a comeback. Already, my arms and legs are lightening, I'm resurging, I'm pink and healthy as a baby.

The nearby mall is so upscale that even the Vendoland janitor is dressed in a bright red blazer. The mall's got the requisite atriums, tinted skylights, fountains, and indoor neo-sidewalk cafés. It's a world-within-the-world; perfect peace and humidity, totally phony, and I love it. The Fiorinal's done its job. My head is vacant and painless.

It must still be raining on the Chief's woodsy acres.

I walk into an art framer's. It's the only empty store and the woman behind the counter, a Buckhead version of Liv Ullmann, with a wide sympathetic face, doesn't seem to mind that I don't look like a serious shopper. I give her my toothiest.

"Just looking," I apologize.

"Why?"

"That's a very reasonable question," I say. She is neatly and expensively dressed; at least, everything looks color coordinated and natural fiberish. She seems many cuts above mall sales assistant.

Besides, Blanquita thinks she's too good for me.

"Don't tell me you have something to frame," she says, laughing. "And I know you wouldn't buy the junk on these walls." She's really a great saleslady. She's narrowed my choices in about ten seconds. She's flattered my tastes. Her eyes are the same greenish blue as her paisley sweater vest.

She's intuitive. It's closing time and it's Sunday, and she opens late on Monday. "But you knew that, didn't you?" she smiles. She helps me out in her amused, laid-back way. Her name is Maura. Thirty-four, divorced, no kids; she gets the statistics out of the way. She's established an easy groundwork. In an hour or two she'll ask those leading questions that are part, more and more, of doing love in the eighties. I check automatically for wedding and friendship rings. The flesh on her ring finger isn't blanched and fluted so I know she's been divorced a while. That's a definite plus. The newly single are to be avoided.

Maura came down from Portland, Oregon, three winters ago. "I don't know why I stay." We're having a pitcher of sangría, still in the mall. I like her voice; it's rueful and teasing. I think I even like her big, sensible hands, so unlike Blanquita's. I spot slivers, chewed nails, nothing glazed or pasted on. Hands that frame the art of Atlanta, such as it is. "Let's see, there's Farmers' Market and the International Airport. What else?"

"The CDC," I protest. The doctors and researchers at the Centers for Disease Control may all be aliens but this is no time to diminish the city's glory. "I'm betting on AIDS to put us on the map." There, I've made it easy, no sweat.

She laughs. I feel witty. I malinger, making small talk. Hard to tell what real time it is, out there in the world, but it must be dark. She suggests we go on to Appleby's on the other side of the mall. Appleby's is perfect for what we have going: relaxed fun and zero sentiment. I've struck gold.

No, I've lost my claim.

We have to drive around to the back of the mall. Her car's a banged-up blue Subaru. Not her fault, she explains; an Oriental sideswiped her just outside Farmers' Market on her first week in Atlanta. She kept the dent and let it rust. Her anti-sunbelt statement.

We order ten-cent oysters for her and Buffalo wings for me and a dollar pitcher. We don't feed each other forkfuls as we might have in a prevenereal era. Afterwards we have to walk around some in the parking lot before finding our way back to her Subaru. I haven't oriented myself to her car yet. It's these little things, first moves, losing the first step, that become so tiring, make me feel I'm slowing down. We've had a pleasant time and what I really want is to let her go.

"Want to hear me play the harpsichord?"

She locates her car key inside her pocketbook. "That's very original," she says. "Should I believe you?"

"Only one way to find out." The harpsichord was part of love's debris. Wendi was musically inclined.

"It's the best line to date," Maura says as she unlocks the door on the passenger side for me.

Sunday night eases into the dark, cozy a.m. of Monday. Maura and I are having ourselves perfect times. The world's a vale of tears only if you keep peering six weeks into the future.

"You're good for me," she keeps whispering, and makes me believe it. "Griff and the Farmers' Market. You're a whole new reason for me to stay."

"We make a good team," I say, knowing I've said it before. I'm already slipping back. I never used a line on Baby, and she never got my jokes anyway. Maura's hair, silvery blond in the condo's dimness, falls over my face. "Partner."

"But we shouldn't talk about it," she says. "That's one of my superstitions."

I feel a small, icy twinge around my heart. I've swallowed too many superstitions these past few months.

Then the phone rings. I lift the phone off the night table and shove it under the bed.

"Oh, Christ, I just knew it," Maura says. "It's too good to be true, isn't it?" I can feel her body tremble. It's the first panic she's displayed.

"Look, I'm ignoring it."

"No you're not."

The ringing stops, waits a while, and starts up again.

"I don't have to answer it." I squeeze her rough hand, then splay the palm flat over my beard. "Give me a smile, pardner."

"It's all right with me," she says in her frank, Northwest way. "You have a life. Your life doesn't begin and end with me." She's

93

already out of bed, already fishing through clothes for the simple things she dropped. "But if you ever need anything framed, do me a big favor, okay?"

The phone keeps up its stop-and-start ringing. It's the Muzak of Purgatory. Maura's dressed in an instant.

"There's no reason why you shouldn't be involved with someone."

Because I can't bear to hear it ring anymore, I shout into the mouthpiece, "What's with you, anyway? You're the one who left!"

But Blanquita the Brave, the giver of two cheers for a new life in a new continent, the pineapple of Joker Rosario's eyes, his Baby, sounds hysterical. I make out phrases. The Chief's into games. The Chief doesn't love her. Oh, Blanquita, you're breaking my heart: don't you know, didn't anyone ever tell you about us? Under it all, you still trust us, you still love. She's calling me from a diner. She's babbling route numbers, gas stations, how to find her. Can t I hear the semis? I'm all she's got.

I hear my voice, loud and insistent. "*Amoco?*" I'm shouting. "There's a hundred Amocos between the perimeter and Chattanooga."

"I don't want to know," I hear Maura tell Marcos as I rush the front door, warm-ups pulled over my pajamas. "I don't want to start anything complicated."

THE
TENANT

MAYA SANYAL has been in Cedar Falls, Iowa, less than two weeks. She's come, books and clothes and one armchair rattling in the smallest truck that U-Haul would rent her, from New Jersey. Before that she was in North Carolina. Before that, Calcutta, India. Every place has something to give. She is sitting at the kitchen table with Fran drinking bourbon for the first time in her life. Fran Johnson found her the furnished apartment and helped her settle in. Now she's brought a bottle of bourbon which gives her the right to stay and talk for a bit. She's breaking up with someone named Vern, a pharmacist. Vern's father is also a pharmacist and owns a drugstore. Maya has seen Vern's father on TV twice already. The first time was on the local news when he spoke out against the selling of painkillers like Advil and Nuprin in supermarkets and gas stations. In the matter of painkillers, Maya is a universalist. The other time he was in a barbershop quartet. Vern gets along all right with his father. He likes the pharmacy business, as business goes, but he wants to go back to graduate school and learn to make films. Maya is drinking her first bourbon tonight because Vern left today for San Francisco State.

"I understand totally," Fran says. She teaches Utopian Fiction and a course in Women's Studies and worked hard to get Maya hired. Maya has a Ph.D. in Comparative Literature and will intoduce writers like R. K. Narayan and Chinua Achebe to three sections of sophomores at the University of Northern Iowa. "A person has to leave home. Try out his wings."

Fran has to use the bathroom. "I don't feel abandoned." She pushes her chair away from the table. "Anyway, it was a sex thing totally. We were good together. It'd be different if I'd loved him."

Maya tries to remember what's in the refrigerator. They need food. She hasn't been to the supermarket in over a week. She doesn't have a car yet and so she relies on a corner store—a longish walk—for milk, cereal, and frozen dinners. Someday these exigencies will show up as bad skin and collapsed muscle tone. No folly is ever lost. Maya pictures history as a net, the kind of safety net travelling trapeze artists of her childhood fell into when they were inattentive, or clumsy. Going to circuses in Calcutta with her father is what she remembers vividly. It is a banal memory, for her father, the owner of a steel company, is a complicated man.

Fran is out in the kitchen long enough for Maya to worry. They need food. Her mother believed in food. What is love, anger, inner peace, etc., her mother used to say, but the brain's biochemistry. Maya doesn't want to get into that, but she is glad she has enough stuff in the refrigerator to make an omelette. She realizes Indian women are supposed to be inventive with food, whip up exotic delights to tickle an American's palate, and she knows she should be meeting Fran's generosity and candor with some sort of bizarre and effortless countermove. If there's an exotic spice store in Cedar Falls or in neighboring Waterloo, she hasn't found it. She's looked in the phone book for common Indian names, especially Bengali, but hasn't yet struck up culinary intimacies. That will come—it always does. There's a six-pack in the fridge that her landlord, Ted Suminski, had put in because she'd be thirsty after unpacking. She was thirsty, but she doesn't drink beer. She probably should have asked him to come up and drink the beer. Except for Fran she hasn't had anyone over. Fran is more friendly and helpful than anyone Maya has known in the States since she came to North Carolina ten years ago, at nineteen. Fran is a Swede, and she is tall, with blue eyes. Her hair, however, is a dull, darkish brown.

"I don't think I can handle anything that heavy-duty," Fran says when she comes back to the room. She means the omelette. "I have to go home in any case." She lives with her mother and her aunt, two women in their mid-seventies, in a drafty farmhouse. The farmhouse now has a computer store catty-corner from it. Maya's been to the farm. She's been shown photographs of the way the corner used to be. If land values ever rebound, Fran will be worth millions.

Before Fran leaves she says, "Has Rab Chatterji called you yet?"

"No." She remembers the name, a good, reliable Bengali name, from the first night's study of the phone book. Dr. Rabindra Chatterji teaches Physics.

"He called the English office just before I left." She takes car keys out of her pocketbook. She reknots her scarf. "I bet Indian men are more sensitive than Americans. Rab's a Brahmin, that's what people say."

A Chatterji has to be a Bengali Brahmin—last names give ancestral secrets away—but Brahminness seems to mean more to Fran than it does to Maya. She was born in 1954, six full years after India became independent. Her India was Nehru's India: a charged, progressive place.

"All Indian men are wife beaters," Maya says. She means it and doesn't mean it. "That's why I married an American." Fran knows about the divorce, but nothing else. Fran is on the Hiring, Tenure, and Reappointment Committee.

Maya sees Fran down the stairs and to the car which is parked in the back in the spot reserved for Maya's car, if she had owned one. It will take her several months to save enough to buy one. She always pays cash, never borrows. She tells herself she's still recovering from the U-Haul drive halfway across the country. Ted Suminski is in his kitchen watching the women. Maya waves to him because waving to him, acknowledging him in that way, makes him seem less creepy. He seems to live alone though a sign, THE SUMINSKIS, hangs from a metal horse's head in the front yard. Maya hasn't seen Mrs. Suminski. She hasn't seen any children either. Ted always looks lonely. When she comes back from campus, he's nearly always in the back, throwing darts or shooting baskets.

"What's he like?" Fran gestures with her head as she starts up her car. "You hear these stories."

Maya doesn't want to know the stories. She has signed a year's lease. She doesn't want complications. "He's all right. I keep out of his way."

"You know what I'm thinking? Of all the people in Cedar Falls, you're the one who could understand Vern best. His wanting to try out his wings, run away, stuff like that."

"Not really." Maya is not being modest. Fran is being impulsively democratic, lumping her wayward lover and Indian friend together as headstrong adventurers. For Fran, a utopian and feminist, borders don't count. Maya's taken some big risks, made a break with her parents' ways. She's done things a woman from Ballygunge Park Road doesn't do, even in fantasies. She's not yet shared stories with Fran, apart from the divorce. She's told her nothing of men she picks up, the reputation she'd gained, before Cedar Falls, for "indiscretions." She has a job, equity, three friends she can count on for emergencies. She is an American citizen. But.

Fran's Brahmin calls her two nights later. On the phone he presents himself as Dr. Chatterji, not Rabindra or Rab. An old-fashioned Indian, she assumes. Her father still calls his closest friend, "Colonel." Dr. Chatterji asks her to tea on Sunday. She means to say no but hears herself saying, "Sunday? Fiveish? I'm not doing anything special this Sunday."

Outside, Ted Suminski is throwing darts into his garage

door. The door has painted-on rings: orange, purple, pink. The bull's-eye is gray. He has to be fifty at least. He is a big, thick, lonely man about whom people tell stories. Maya pulls the phone cord as far as it'll go so she can look down more directly on her landlord's large, bald head. He has his back to her as he lines up a dart. He's in black running shoes, red shorts, he's naked to the waist. He hunches his right shoulder, he pulls the arm back; a big, lonely man shouldn't have so much grace. The dart is ready to cut through the September evening. But Ted Suminski doesn't let go. He swings on worn rubber soles, catches her eye in the window (she has to have imagined this), takes aim at her shadow. Could she have imagined the noise of the dart's metal tip on her windowpane?

Dr. Chatterji is still on the phone. "You are not having any mode of transportation, is that right?"

Ted Suminski has lost interest in her. Perhaps it isn't interest, at all; perhaps it's aggression. "I don't drive," she lies, knowing it sounds less shameful than not owning a car. She has said this so often she can get in the right degree of apology and Asian upper-class helplessness. "It's an awful nuisance."

"Not to worry, please." Then, "It is a great honor to be meeting Dr. Sanyal's daughter. In Calcutta business circles he is a legend."

On Sunday she is ready by four-thirty. She doesn't know what the afternoon holds; there are surely no places for "high tea"—a colonial tradition—in Cedar Falls, Iowa. If he takes her back to his place, it will mean he has invited other guests. From his voice she can tell Dr. Chatterji likes to do things correctly. She has dressed herself in a peach-colored nylon georgette sari, jade drop-earrings and a necklace. The color is good on dark skin. She is not pretty, but she does her best. Working at it is a part of self-respect. In the mid-seventies, when American women felt rather strongly about such things, Maya had been in trouble with her women's group at Duke. She was too feminine. She had tried to explain the world she came out of.

Her grandmother had been married off at the age of five in a village now in Bangladesh. Her great-aunt had been burned to death over a dowry problem. She herself had been trained to speak softly, arrange flowers, sing, be pliant. If she were to seduce Ted Suminski, she thinks as she waits in the front yard for Dr. Chatterji, it would be minor heroism. She has broken with the past. But.

Dr. Chatterji drives up for her at about five ten. He is a hesitant driver. The car stalls, jumps ahead, finally slams to a stop. Maya has to tell him to back off a foot or so; it's hard to leap over two sacks of pruned branches in a sari. Ted Suminski is an obsessive pruner and gardener.

"My sincerest apologies, Mrs. Sanyal," Dr. Chatterji says. He leans across the wide front seat of his noisy, very old, very used car and unlocks the door for her. "I am late. But then, I am sure you're remembering that Indian Standard Time is not at all the same as time in the States." He laughs. He could be nervous—she often had that effect on Indian men. Or he could just be chatty. "These Americans are all the time rushing and rushing but where it gets them?" He moves his head laterally once, twice. It's the gesture made famous by Peter Sellers. When Peter Sellers did it, it had seemed hilarious. Now it suggests that Maya and Dr. Chatterji have three thousand years plus civilization, sophistication, moral virtue, over people born on this continent. Like her, Dr. Chatterji is a naturalized American.

"Call me Maya," she says. She fusses with the seat belt. She does it because she needs time to look him over. He seems quite harmless. She takes in the prominent teeth, the eyebrows that run together. He's in a blue shirt and a beige cardigan with the K-Mart logo that buttons tightly over the waist. It's hard to guess his age because he has dyed his hair and his moustache. Late thirties, early forties. Older than she had expected. "Not Mrs. Sanyal."

This isn't the time to tell about ex-husbands. She doesn't know where John is these days. He should have kept up at least.

John had come into her life as a graduate student at Duke, and she, mistaking the brief breathlessness of sex for love, had married him. They had stayed together two years, maybe a little less. The pain that John had inflicted all those years ago by leaving her had subsided into a cozy feeling of loss. This isn't the time, but then she doesn't want to be a legend's daughter all evening. She's not necessarily on Dr. Chatterji's side is what she wants to get across early; she's not against America and Americans. She makes the story—of marriage outside the Brahminic pale, the divorce—quick, dull. Her unsentimentality seems to shock him. His stomach sags inside the cardigan.

"We've each had our several griefs," the physicist. says. "We're each required to pay our karmic debts."

"Where are we headed?"

"Mrs. Chatterji has made some Indian snacks. She is waiting to meet you because she is knowing your cousin-sister who studied in Scottish Church College. My home is okay, no?"

Fran would get a kick out of this. Maya has slept with married men, with nameless men, with men little more than boys, but never with an Indian man. Never.

The Chatterjis live in a small blue house on a gravelly street. There are at least five or six other houses on the street; the same size but in different colors and with different front yard treatments. More houses are going up. This is the cutting edge of suburbia.

Mrs. Chatterji stands in the driveway. She is throwing a large plastic ball to a child. The child looks about four, and is Korean or Cambodian. The child is not hers because she tells it, "Chung-Hee, ta-ta, bye-bye. Now I play with guest," as Maya gets out of the car.

Maya hasn't seen this part of town. The early September light softens the construction pits. In that light the houses too close together, the stout woman in a striped cotton sari, the child hugging a pink ball, the two plastic lawn chairs by a tender young tree, the sheets and saris on the clothesline in the back, all seem miraculously incandescent.

"Go home now, Chung-Hee. I am busy." Mrs. Chatterji points the child homeward, then turns to Maya, who has folded her hands in traditional Bengali greeting. "It is an honor. We feel very privileged." She leads Maya indoors to a front room that smells of moisture and paint.

In her new, deliquescent mood, Maya allows herself to be backed into the best armchair—a low-backed, boxy Goodwill item draped over with a Rajasthani bedspread—and asks after the cousin Mrs. Chatterji knows. She doesn't want to let go of Mrs. Chatterji. She doesn't want husband and wife to get into whispered conferences about their guest's misadventures in America, as they make tea in the kitchen.

The coffee table is already laid with platters of mutton croquettes, fish chops, onion pakoras, ghugni with puris, samosas, chutneys. Mrs. Chatterji has gone to too much trouble. Maya counts four kinds of sweetmeats in Corning casseroles on an end table. She looks into a see-through lid; spongy, white dumplings float in rosewater syrup. Planets contained, mysteries made visible.

"What are you waiting for, Santana?" Dr. Chatterji becomes imperious, though not unaffectionate. He pulls a dining chair up close to the coffee table. "Make some tea." He speaks in Bengali to his wife, in English to Maya. To Maya he says, grandly, "We are having real Indian Green Label Lipton. A nephew is bringing it just one month back."

His wife ignores him. "The kettle's already on," she says. She wants to know about the Sanyal family. Is it true her great-grandfather was a member of the Star Chamber in England?

Nothing in Calcutta is ever lost. Just as her story is known to Bengalis all over America, so are the scandals of her family, the grandfather hauled up for tax evasion, the aunt who left her husband to act in films. This woman brings up the Star Chamber, the glories of the Sanyal family, her father's philanthropies, but it's a way of saying, *I know the dirt*.

The bedrooms are upstairs. In one of those bedrooms an unseen, tormented presence—Maya pictures it as a clumsy ghost that strains to shake off the body's shell—drops things on the floor. The things are heavy and they make the front room's chandelier shake. Light bulbs, shaped like tiny candle flames, flicker. The Chatterjis have said nothing about children. There are no tricycles in the hallway, no small sandals behind the doors. Maya is too polite to ask about the noise, and the Chatterjis don't explain. They talk just a little louder. They flip the embroidered cover off the stereo. What would Maya like to hear? Hemanta Kumar? Manna Dey? Oh, that young chap, Manna Dey! What sincerity, what tenderness he can convey!

Upstairs the ghost doesn't hear the music of nostalgia. The ghost throws and thumps. The ghost makes its own vehement music. Maya hears in its voice madness, self-hate.

Finally the water in the kettle comes to a boil. The whistle cuts through all fantasy and pretense. Dr. Chatterji says, "I'll see to it," and rushes out of the room. But he doesn't go to the kitchen. He shouts up the stairwell. "Poltoo, kindly stop this nonsense straightaway! We're having a brilliant and cultured lady-guest and you're creating earthquakes?" The kettle is hysterical.

Mrs. Chatterji wipes her face. The face that had seemed plump and cheery at the start of the evening now is flabby. "My sister's boy," the woman says.

So this is the nephew who has brought with him the cartons of Green Label tea, one of which will be given to Maya.

Mrs. Chatterji speaks to Maya in English as though only the alien language can keep emotions in check. "Such an intelligent boy! His father is government servant. Very highly placed."

Maya is meant to visualize a smart, clean-cut young man from south Calcutta, but all she can see is a crazy, thwarted, lost graduate student. Intelligence, proper family guarantee nothing. Even Brahmins can do self-destructive things, feel unsavory urges. Maya herself had been an excellent student.

"He was First Class First in B. Sc. from Presidency College," the woman says. "Now he's getting Master's in Ag. Science at Iowa State."

The kitchen is silent Dr. Chatterji comes back into the room with a tray. The teapot is under a tea cozy, a Kashmiri one embroidered with the usual chinar leaves, loops, and chains. "*Her* nephew," he says. The dyed hair and dyed moustache are no longer signs of a man wishing to fight the odds. He is a vain man, anxious to cut losses. "Very unfortunate business."

The nephew's story comes out slowly, over fish chops and mutton croquettes. He is in love with a student from Ghana.

"Everything was A-Okay until the Christmas break. Grades, assistantship for next semester, everything."

"I blame the college. The office for foreign students arranged a Christmas party. And now, *baapre baap!* Our poor Poltoo wants to marry a Negro Muslim."

Maya is known for her nasty, ironic one-liners. It has taken her friends weeks to overlook her malicious, un-American plea-sure in others' misfortunes. Maya would like to finish Dr. Chatterji off quickly. He is pompous; he is reactionary; he wants to live and work in America but give back nothing except taxes. The confused world of the immigrant—the lostness that Maya and Poltoo feel—that's what Dr. Chatterji wants to avoid. She hates him. But.

Dr. Chatterji's horror is real. A good Brahmin boy in Iowa is in love with an African Muslim. It shouldn't be a big deal. But the more she watches the physicist, the more she realizes that "Brahmin" isn't a caste; it's a metaphor. You break one small rule, and the constellation collapses. She thinks suddenly that John Cheever—she is teaching him as a "world writer" in her classes, cheek-by-jowl with Africans and West Indians—would have understood Dr. Chatterji's dread. Cheever had been on her mind, ever since the late afternoon light slanted over Mrs. Chatterji's drying saris. She remembers now how full of a soft, Cheeverian light Durham had been the summer she had slept with John Hadwen; and how after that, her tidy graduate-student world became monstrous, lawless. All men became

John Hadwen; John became all men. Outwardly, she retained her poise, her Brahminical breeding. She treated her crisis as a literary event; she lost her moral sense, her judgment, her power to distinguish. Her parents had behaved magnanimously. They had cabled from Calcutta: WHAT'S DONE IS DONE. WE ARE CONFIDENT YOU WILL HANDLE NEW SITUATIONS WELL. ALL LOVE. But she knows more than do her parents. Love is anarchy.

Poltoo is Mrs. Chatterji's favorite nephew. She looks as though it is her fault that the Sunday has turned unpleasant. She stacks the empty platters methodically. To Maya she says, "It is the goddess who pulls the strings. We are puppets. I know the goddess will fix it. Poltoo will not marry that African woman." Then she goes to the coat closet in the hall and staggers back with a harmonium, the kind sold in music stores in Calcutta, and sets it down on the carpeted floor. "We're nothing but puppets," she says again. She sits at Maya's feet, her pudgy hands on the harmonium's shiny, black bellows. She sings, beautifully, in a virgin's high voice, "Come, goddess, come, muse, come to us hapless peoples' rescue."

Maya is astonished. She has taken singing lessons at Dakshini Academy in Calcutta. She plays the sitar and the tanpur, well enough to please Bengalis, to astonish Americans. But stout Mrs. Chatterji is a devotee, talking to God.

A little after eight, Dr. Chatterji drops her off. It's been an odd evening and they are both subdued.

"I want to say one thing," he says. He stops her from undoing her seat belt. The plastic sacks of pruned branches are still at the corner.

"You don't have to get out," she says.

"Please. Give me one more minute of your time."

"Sure."

"Maya is my favorite name."

She says nothing. She turns away from him without making her embarrassment obvious.

"Truly speaking, it is my favorite. You are sometimes lonely, no? But you are lucky. Divorced women can date, they can go to bars and discos. They can see mens, many mens. But inside marriage there is so much loneliness." A groan, low, horrible, comes out of him.

She turns back toward him, to unlatch the seat belt and run out of the car. She sees that Dr. Chatterji's pants are unzipped. One hand works hard under his Jockey shorts; the other rests, limp, penitential, on the steering wheel.

"Dr. Chatterji—*really!*" she cries.

The next day, Monday, instead of getting a ride home with Fran—Fran says she *likes* to give rides, she needs the chance to talk, and she won't share gas expenses, absolutely not—Maya goes to the periodicals room of the library. There are newspapers from everywhere, even from Madagascar and New Caledonia. She thinks of the periodicals room as an asylum for homesick aliens. There are two aliens already in the room, both Orientals, both absorbed in the politics and gossip of their far off homes.

She goes straight to the newspapers from India. She bunches her raincoat like a bolster to make herself more comfortable. There's so much to catch up on. A village headman, a known Congress-Indira party worker, has been shot at by scooter-riding snipers. An Indian pugilist has won an international medal—in Nepal. A child drawing well water—the reporter calls the child "a neo-Buddhist, a convert from the now-outlawed untouchable caste"—has been stoned. An editorial explains that the story about stoning is not a story about caste but about failed idealism; a story about promises of green fields and clean, potable water broken, a story about bribes paid and wells not dug. But no, thinks Maya, it's about caste.

Out here, in the heartland of the new world, the India of serious newspapers unsettles. Maya longs again to feel what she had felt in the Chatterjis' living room: virtues made physical. It is a familiar feeling, a longing. Had a suitable man presented himself in the reading room at that instant, she would have seduced him. She goes on to the stack of *India Abroads*, reads through matrimonial columns, and steals an issue to take home.

Indian men want Indian brides. Married Indian men want Indian mistresses. All over America, "handsome, tall, fair" engineers, doctors, data processors—the new pioneers—cry their eerie love calls.

Maya runs a finger down the first column; her fingertip, dark with newsprint, stops at random.

Hello! Hi! Yes, you *are* the one I'm looking for. You are the new emancipated Indo-American woman. You have a zest for life. You are at ease in USA and yet your ethics are rooted in Indian tradition. The man of your dreams has come. Yours truly is handsome, ear-nose-throat specialist, well-settled in Connecticut. Age is 41 but never married, physically fit, sportsmanly, and strong. I adore idealism, poetry, beauty. I abhor smugness, passivity, caste system. Write with recent photo. Better still, call!!!

Maya calls. Hullo, hullo, hullo! She hears immigrant lovers cry in crowded shopping malls. Yes, you who are at ease in both worlds, you are the one. She feels she has a fair chance.

A man answers. "Ashoke Mehta speaking."

She speaks quickly into the bright-red mouthpiece of her telephone. He will be in Chicago, in transit, passing through O'Hare. United counter, Saturday, two p.m. As easy as that.

"Good," Ashoke Mehta says. "For these encounters I, too, prefer a neutral zone."

On Saturday at exactly two o'clock the man of Maya's dreams floats toward her as lovers used to in shampoo commercials. The United counter is a loud, harrassed place but passengers and piled-up luggage fall away from him. Full-cheeked and fleshy-lipped, he is handsome. He hasn't lied. He is serene, assured, a Hindu god touching down in Illinois.

She can't move. She feels ugly and unworthy. Her adult life no longer seems miraculously rebellious; it is grim, it is perverse. She has accomplished nothing. She has changed her citizenship but she hasn't broken through into the light, the vigor, the *hustle* of the New World. She is stuck in dead space.

"Hullo, Hullo!" Their fingers touch.

Oh, the excitement! Ashoke Mehta's palm feels so right in the small of her back. Hullo, hullo, hullo. He pushes her out of the reach of anti-Khomeini Iranians, Hare Krishnas, American Fascists, men with fierce wants, and guides her to an empty gate. They have less than an hour.

"What would you like, Maya?"

She knows he can read her mind, she knows her thoughts are open to him. *You*, she's almost giddy with the thought, with simple desire. "From the snack bar," he says, as though to clarify. "I'm afraid I'm starved."

Below them, where the light is strong and hurtful, a Boeing is being serviced. "Nothing," she says.

He leans forward. She can feel the nap of his scarf—she recognizes the Cambridge colors—she can smell the wool of his Icelandic sweater. She runs her hand along the scarf, then against the flesh of his neck. "Only the impulsive ones call," he says.

The immigrant courtship proceeds. It's easy, he's good with facts. He knows how to come across to a stranger who may end up a lover, a spouse. He makes over a hundred thousand. He owns a house in Hartford, and two income properties in Newark. He plays the market but he's cautious. He's good at badminton but plays handball to keep in shape. He watches all the sports on television. Last August he visited Copenhagen, Helsinki and Leningrad. Once upon a time he collected stamps but now he doesn't have hobbies, except for reading. He counts himself an intellectual, he spends too much on books. Ludlum, Forsyth, MacInnes; other names she doesn't catch. She supresses a smile, she's told him only she's a graduate student. He's not without his vices. He's a spender, not a saver. He's a sensualist: good food—all foods, but easy on the Indian—good wine. Some temptations he doesn't try to resist.

And I, she wants to ask, do I tempt?

"Now tell me about yourself, Maya." He makes it easy for her. "Have you ever been in love?"

"No."

"But many have loved you, I can see that." He says it not unkindly. It is the fate of women like her, and men like him. Their karmic duty, to be loved. It is expected, not judged. She feels he can see them all, the sad parade of need and demand. This isn't the time to reveal all.

And so the courtship enters a second phase.

When she gets back to Cedar Falls, Ted Suminski is standing on the front porch. It's late at night, chilly. He is wearing a down vest. She's never seen him on the porch. In fact there's no chair to sit on. He looks chilled through. He's waited around a while.

"Hi." She has her keys ready. This isn't the night to offer the six-pack in the fridge. He looks expectant, ready to pounce.

"Hi." He looks like a man who might have aimed the dart at her. What has he done to his wife, his kids? Why isn't there at least a dog? "Say, I left a note upstairs."

The note is written in Magic Marker and thumb-tacked to her apartment door. DUE TO PERSONAL REASONS, NAMELY REMARRIAGE, I REQUEST THAT YOU VACATE MY PLACE AT THE END OF THE SEMESTER.

Maya takes the note down and retacks it to the kitchen wall. The whole wall is like a bulletin board, made of some new, crumbly building-material. Her kitchen, Ted Suminski had told her, was once a child's bedroom. Suminski in love: the idea stuns her. She has misread her landlord. The dart at her window speaks of no twisted fantasy. The landlord wants the tenant out.

She gets a glass out of the kitchen cabinet, gets out a tray of ice, pours herself a shot of Fran's bourbon. She is happy for Ted Suminski. She is. She wants to tell someone how moved she'd been by Mrs. Chatterji's singing. How she'd felt in O'Hare, even about Dr. Rab Chatterji in the car. But Fran is not the person. No one she's ever met is the person. She can't talk about the dead space she lives in. She wishes Ashoke Mehta would call. Right now.

Weeks pass. Then two months. She finds a new room, signs another lease. Her new landlord calls himself Fred. He has no arms, but he helps her move her things. He drives between Ted Suminski's place and his twice in his station wagon. He uses his toes the way Maya uses her fingers. He likes to do things. He pushes garbage sacks full of Maya's clothes up the stairs.

"It's all right to stare," Fred says. "Hell, I would."

That first afternoon in Fred's rooming house, they share a Chianti. Fred wants to cook her pork chops but he's a little shy about Indians and meat. Is it beef, or pork? Or any meat? She says it's okay, any meat, but not tonight. He has an ex-wife in Des Moines, two kids in Portland, Oregon. The kids are both normal; he's the only freak in the family. But he's self-reliant. He shops in the supermarket like anyone else, he carries out the garbage, shovels the snow off the sidewalk. He needs Maya's help with one thing. Just one thing. The box of Tide is a bit too heavy to manage. Could she get him the giant size every so often and leave it in the basement?

The dead space need not suffocate. Over the months, Fred and she will settle into companionship. She has never slept with a man without arms. Two wounded people, he will joke during their nightly contortions. It will shock her, this assumed equivalence with a man so strikingly deficient. She knows she is strange, and lonely, but being Indian is not the same, she would have thought, as being a freak.

One night in spring, Fred's phone rings. "Ashoke Mehta speaking." None of this "do you remember me?" nonsense.

The god has tracked her down. He hasn't forgotten. "Hullo," he says, in their special way. And because she doesn't answer back, "Hullo, hullo, hullo." She is aware of Fred in the back of the room. He is lighting a cigarette with his toes.

"Yes," she says, "I remember."

"I had to take care of a problem," Ashoke Mehta says. "You know that I have my vices. That time at O'Hare I was honest with you."

She is breathless.

"Who is it, May?" asks Fred.

"You also have a problem," says the voice. His laugh echoes. "You will come to Hartford, I know."

When she moves out, she tells herself, it will not be the end of Fred's world.

FATHERING

ENG stands just inside our bedroom door, her fidgety fist on the doorknob which Sharon, in a sulk, polished to a gleam yesterday afternoon.

"I'm starved," she says.

I know a sick little girl when I see one. I brought the twins up without much help ten years ago. Eng's got a high fever. Brownish stains stiffen the nap of her terry robe. Sour smells fill the bedroom.

"For God's sake leave us alone," Sharon mutters under the quilt. She turns away from me. We bought the quilt at a garage sale in Rock Springs the Sunday two years ago when she moved in. "Talk to her."

Sharon works on this near-marriage of ours. I'll hand it to her, she really does. I knead her shoulders, and I say, "Easy, easy," though I really hate it when she treats Eng like a deaf-mute. "My girl speaks English, remember?"

Eng can outcuss any freckle-faced kid on the block. Someone in the killing fields must have taught her. Maybe her mama, the honeyest-skinned bar girl with the tiniest feet in Saigon. I was an errand boy with the Combined Military Intelligence. I did the whole war on Dexedrine. Vietnam didn't happen, and I'd put it behind me in marriage and fatherhood and teaching high

117

school. Ten years later came the screw-ups with the marriage, the job, women, the works. Until Eng popped up in my life, I really believed it didn't happen.

"Come here, sweetheart," I beg my daughter. I sidle closer to Sharon, so there'll be room under the quilt for Eng.

"I'm starved," she complains from the doorway. She doesn't budge. The robe and hair are smelling something fierce. She doesn't show any desire to cuddle. She must be sick. She must have thrown up all night. Sharon throws the quilt back. "Then go raid the refrigerator like a normal kid," she snaps.

Once upon a time Sharon used to be a cheerful, accommodating woman. It isn't as if Eng was dumped on us out of the blue. She knew I was tracking my kid. Coming to terms with the past was Sharon's idea. I don't know what happened to *that* Sharon. "For all you know, Jason," she'd said, "the baby died of malaria or something." She said, "Go on, find out and deal with it." She said she could handle being a stepmother—better a fresh chance with some orphan off the streets of Saigon than with my twins from Rochester. My twins are being raised in some organic-farming lesbo commune. Their mother breeds Nubian goats for a living. "Come get in bed with us, baby. Let Dad feel your forehead. You burning up with fever?"

"She isn't hungry, I think she's sick," I tell Sharon, but she's already tugging her sleeping mask back on. "I think she's just letting us know she hurts."

I hold my arms out wide for Eng to run into. If I could, I'd suck the virus right out of her. In the jungle, VC mamas used to do that. Some nights we'd steal right up to a hootch—just a few of us intense sons of bitches on some special mission—and the women would be at their mumbo jumbo. They'd be sticking coins and amulets into napalm burns.

"I'm hungry, Dad." It comes out as a moan. Okay, she doesn't run into my arms, but at least she's come as far in as the foot of our bed. "Dad, let's go down to the kitchen. Just you and me."

I am about to let that pass though I can feel Sharon's body go into weird little jerks and twitches when my baby adds with emphatic viciousness, "Not her, Dad. We don't want her with us in the kitchen."

"She loves you," I protest. Love—not spite—makes Eng so territorial; that's what I want to explain to Sharon. She's a sick, frightened, foreign kid, for Chrissake. "Don't you, Sharon? Sharon's concerned about you."

But Sharon turns over on her stomach. "You know what's wrong with you, Jase? You can't admit you're being manipulated. You can't cut through the 'frightened-foreign-kid' shit."

Eng moves closer. She comes up to the side of my bed, but doesn't touch the hand I'm holding out. She's a fighter.

"I feel fire-hot, Dad. My bones feel pain."

"Sharon?" I want to deserve this woman. "Sharon, I'm so sorry." It isn't anybody's fault. You need uppers to get through peace times, too.

"Dad. Let's go. Chop-chop."

"You're too sick to keep food down, baby. Curl up in here. Just for a bit?"

"I'd throw up, Dad."

"I'll carry you back to your room. I'll read you a story, okay?"

Eng watches me real close as I pull the quilt off. "You got any scars you haven't shown me yet? My mom had a big scar on one leg. Shrapnel. Boom boom. I got scars. See? I got lots of bruises."

I scoop up my poor girl and rush her, terry robe flapping, to her room which Sharon fixed up with white girlish furniture in less complicated days. Waiting for Eng was good. Sharon herself said it was good for our relationship. "Could you bring us some juice and aspirin?" I shout from the hallway.

"Aspirin isn't going to cure Eng," I hear Sharon yell. "I'm going to call Dr. Kearns."

Downstairs I hear Sharon on the phone. She isn't talking flu viruses. She's talking social workers and shrinks. My girl isn't crazy; she's picked up a bug in school as might anyone else.

"The child's arms are covered with bruises," Sharon is saying. "Nothing major. They look like . . . well, they're sort of tiny circles and welts." There's nothing for a while. Then she says, "Christ! no, Jason can't do enough for her! That's not what I'm saying! What's happening to this country? You think we're perverts? What I'm saying is the girl's doing it to herself."

"Who are you talking to?" I ask from the top of the stairs. "What happened to the aspirin?"

I lean as far forward over the railing as I dare so I can see what Sharon's up to. She's getting into her coat and boots. She's having trouble with buttons and snaps. In the bluish light of the foyer's broken chandelier, she looks old, harrowed, depressed. What have I done to her?

"What's going on?" I plead. "You deserting me?"

"Don't be so fucking melodramatic. I'm going to the mall to buy some aspirin."

"How come we don't have any in the house?"

"Why are you always picking on me?"

"Who was that on the phone?"

"So now you want me to account for every call and every trip?" She ties an angry knot into her scarf. But she tells me. "I was talking to Meg Kearns. She says Dr. Kearns has gone hunting for the day."

"Great!"

"She says he has his beeper on him."

I hear the back door stick and Sharon swear. She's having trouble with the latch. "Jiggle it gently," I shout, taking the stairs two at a time. But before I can come down, her Nissan backs out of the parking apron.

Back upstairs I catch Eng in the middle of a dream or delirium. "They got Grandma!" she screams. She goes very rigid in bed. It's a four-poster with canopy and ruffles and stuff that Sharon put on her MasterCard. The twins slept on bunk beds.

With the twins it was different, totally different. Dr. Spock can't be point man for Eng, for us.

"She bring me food," Eng's screaming. "She bring me food from the forest. They shoot Grandma! Bastards!"

"Eng?" I don't dare touch her. I don't know how.

"You shoot my grandmother?" She whacks the air with her bony arms. Now I see the bruises, the small welts all along the insides of her arms. Some have to be weeks old, they're that yellow. The twins' scrapes and cuts never turned that ochre. I can't help wondering if maybe Asian skin bruises differently from ours, even though I want to say skin is skin; especially hers is skin like mine.

"I want to be with Grandma. Grandma loves me. I want to be ghost. I don't want to get better."

I read to her. I read to her because good parents are supposed to read to their kids laid up sick in bed. I want to do it right. I want to be a good father. I read from a sci-fi novel that Sharon must have picked up. She works in a camera store in the mall, right next to a B. Dalton. I read three pages out loud, then I read four chapters to myself because Eng's stopped up her ears. Aliens have taken over small towns all over the country. Idaho, Nebraska: no state is safe from aliens.

Some time after two, the phone rings. Since Sharon doesn't answer it on the second ring, I know she isn't back. She carries a cordless phone everywhere around the house. In the movies, when cops have bad news to deliver, they lean on your doorbell; they don't call. Sharon will come back when she's ready. We'll make up. Things will get back to normal.

"Jason?"

I know Dr. Kearns's voice. He saw the twins through the usual immunizations.

"I have Sharon here. She'll need a ride home. Can you drive over?"

"God! What's happened?"

"Nothing to panic about. Nothing physical. She came for a consultation."

"Give me a half-hour. I have to wrap Eng real warm so I can drag her out in this miserable weather."

"Take your time. This way I can take a look at Eng, too."

"What's wrong with Sharon?"

"She's a little exercised about a situation. I gave her a sedative. See you in a half-hour."

I ease delirious Eng out of the overdecorated four-poster, prop her against my body while I wrap a blanket around her. She's a tiny thing, but she feels stiff and heavy, a sleepwalking mummy. Her eyes are dry-bright, strange.

It's a sunny winter day, and the evergreens in the front yard are glossy with frost. I press Eng against my chest as I negotiate the front steps. Where the gutter leaks, the steps feel spongy. The shrubs and bushes my ex-wife planted clog the front path. I've put twenty years into this house. The steps, the path, the house all have a right to fall apart.

I'm thirty-eight. I've let a lot of people down already.

The inside of the van is deadly cold. Mid-January ice mottles the windshield. I lay the bundled-up child on the long seat behind me and wait for the engine to warm up. It feels good with the radio going and the heat coming on. I don't want the ice on the windshield to melt. Eng and I are safest in the van.

In the rear-view mirror, Eng's wrinkled lips begin to move. "Dad, can I have a quarter?"

"May I, kiddo," I joke.

There's all sorts of junk in the pockets of my parka. Buckshot, dimes and quarters for the vending machine, a Blistex.

"What do you need it for, sweetheart?"

Eng's quick. Like the street kids in Saigon who dove for cigarettes and sticks of gum. She's loosened the blanket folds around her. I watch her tuck the quarter inside her wool mitt. She grins. "Thanks, soldier."

At Dr. Kearns's, Sharon is lying unnaturally slack-bodied on the lone vinyl sofa. Her coat's neatly balled up under her neck, like a bolster. Right now she looks amiable, docile. I don't think she exactly recognizes me, although later she'll say she did. All that stuff about Kearns going hunting must have been a lie. Even the stuff about having to buy aspirins in the mall. She was planning all along to get here.

"What's wrong?"

"It's none of my business, Jason, but you and Sharon might try an honest-to-goodness heart-to-heart." Then he makes a sign to me to lay Eng on the examining table. "We don't look so bad," he says to my daughter. Then he excuses himself and goes into a glass-walled cubicle.

Sharon heaves herself into a sitting position of sorts on the sofa. "Everything was fine until she got here. Send her back, Jase. If you love me, send her back." She's slouched so far forward, her pointed, sweatered breasts nearly touch her corduroy pants. She looks helpless, pathetic. I've brought her to this state. Guilt, not love, is what I feel.

I want to comfort Sharon, but my daughter with the wild, grieving pygmy face won't let go of my hand. "She's bad, Dad. Send *her* back."

Dr. Kearns comes out of the cubicle balancing a sample bottle of pills or caplets on a flattened palm. He has a boxer's tough, squarish hands. "Miraculous stuff, this," he laughs. "But first we'll stick our tongue out and say *ahh*. Come on, open wide."

Eng opens her mouth real wide, then brings her teeth together, hard, on Dr. Kearns's hand. She leaps erect on the examining table, tearing the disposable paper sheet with her toes. Her tiny, funny toes are doing a frantic dance. "Don't let him touch me, Grandma!"

"He's going to make you all better, baby." I can't pull my alien child down, I can't comfort her. The twins had diseases with easy names, diseases we knew what to do with. The thing is, I never felt for them what I feel for her.

"Don't let him touch me, Grandma!" Eng's screaming now. She's hopping on the table and screaming. "Kill him, Grandma! Get me out of here, Grandma!"

"Baby, it's all right."

But she looks through me and the country doctor as though we aren't here, as though we aren't pulling at her to make her lie down.

"Lie back like a good girl," Dr. Kearns commands.

But Eng is listening to other voices. She pulls her mitts off with her teeth, chucks the blanket, the robe, the pajamas to the floor; then, naked, hysterical, she presses the quarter I gave her deep into the soft flesh of her arm. She presses and presses that coin, turning it in nasty half-circles until blood starts to pool under the skin.

"Jason, grab her at the knees. Get her back down on the table."

From the sofa, Sharon moans. "See, I told you the child was crazy. She hates me. She's possessive about Jason."

The doctor comes at us with his syringe. He's sedated Sharon; now he wants to knock out my kid with his cures.

"Get the hell out, you bastard!" Eng yells. "*Vamos!* Bang bang!" She's pointing her arm like a semiautomatic, taking out Sharon, then the doctor. My Rambo. "Old way is good way. Money cure is good cure. When they shoot my grandma, you think pills do her any good? You Yankees, please go home." She looks straight at me. "Scram, Yankee bastard!"

Dr. Kearns has Eng by the wrist now. He has flung the quarter I gave her on the floor. Something incurable is happening to my women.

Then, as in fairy tales, I know what has to be done. "Coming, pardner!" I whisper. "I got no end of coins." I jiggle the change in my pocket. I jerk her away from our enemies. My Saigon kid and me: we're a team. In five minutes we'll be safely away in the cold chariot of our van.

__JASMINE__

JASMINE came to Detroit from Port-of-Spain, Trinidad, by way of Canada. She crossed the border at Windsor in the back of a gray van loaded with mattresses and box springs. The plan was for her to hide in an empty mattress box if she heard the driver say, "All bad weather seems to come down from Canada, doesn't it?" to the customs man. But she didn't have to crawl into a box and hold her breath. The customs man didn't ask to look in.

The driver let her off at a scary intersection on Woodward Avenue and gave her instructions on how to get to the Plantations Motel in Southfield. The trick was to keep changing vehicles, he said. That threw off the immigration guys real quick.

Jasmine took money for cab fare out of the pocket of the great big raincoat that the van driver had given her. The raincoat looked like something that nuns in Port-of-Spain sold in church bazaars. Jasmine was glad to have a coat with wool lining, though; and anyway, who would know in Detroit that she was Dr. Vassanji's daughter?

All the bills in her hand looked the same. She would have to be careful when she paid the cabdriver. Money in Detroit wasn't pretty the way it was back home, or even in Canada, but she liked this money better. Why should money be pretty, like a picture? Pretty money is only good for putting on your walls maybe. The dollar bills felt businesslike, serious. Back home at work, she used to count out thousands of Trinidad dollars every day and not even think of them as real. Real money was worn and green, American dollars. Holding the bills in her fist on a street corner meant she had made it in okay. She'd outsmarted the guys at the border. Now it was up to her to use her wits to do something with her life. As her Daddy kept saying, "Girl, is opportunity come only once." The girls she'd worked with at the bank in Port-of-Spain had gone green as bananas when she'd walked in with her ticket on Air Canada. Trinidad was too tiny. That was the trouble. Trinidad was an island stuck in the middle of nowhere. What kind of place was that for a girl with ambition?

The Plantations Motel was run by a family of Trinidad Indians who had come from the tuppenny-ha'penny country town, Chaguanas. The Daboos were nobodies back home. They were lucky, that's all. They'd gotten here before the rush and bought up a motel and an ice cream parlor. Jasmine felt very superior when she saw Mr. Daboo in the motel's reception area. He was a pumpkin-shaped man with very black skin and Elvis Presley sideburns turning white. They looked like earmuffs. Mrs. Daboo was a bumpkin, too; short, fat, flapping around in house slippers. The Daboo daughters seemed very American, though. They didn't seem to know that they were nobodies, and kept looking at her and giggling.

She knew she would be short of cash for a great long while. Besides, she wasn't sure she wanted to wear bright leather boots and leotards like Viola and Loretta. The smartest move she could make would be to put a down payment on a husband. Her Daddy had told her to talk to the Daboos first chance. The Daboos ran a service fixing up illegals with islanders who had made it in legally. Daddy had paid three thousand back in Trinidad, with the Daboos and the mattress man getting part of it. They should throw in a good-earning husband for that kind of money.

The Daboos asked her to keep books for them and to clean the rooms in the new wing, and she could stay in 16B as long as she liked. They showed her 16B. They said she could cook her own roti; Mr. Daboo would bring in a stove, two gas rings that you could fold up in a metal box. The room was quite grand, Jasmine thought. It had a double bed, a TV, a pink sink and matching bathtub. Mrs. Daboo said Jasmine wasn't the big-city Port-of-Spain type she'd expected. Mr. Daboo said that he wanted her to stay because it was nice to have a neat, cheerful person around. It wasn't a bad deal, better than stories she'd heard about Trinidad girls in the States.

All day every day except Sundays Jasmine worked. There wasn't just the bookkeeping and the cleaning up. Mr. Daboo had her working on the match-up marriage service. Jasmine's job was to check up on social security cards, call clients' bosses for references, and make sure credit information wasn't false. Dermatologists and engineers living in Bloomfield Hills, store owners on Canfield and Woodward: she treated them all as potential liars. One of the first things she learned was that Ann Arbor was a magic word. A boy goes to Ann Arbor and gets an education, and all the barriers come crashing down. So Ann Arbor was the place to be.

She didn't mind the work. She was learning about Detroit, every side of it. Sunday mornings she helped unload packing crates of Caribbean spices in a shop on the next block. For the first time in her life, she was working for a black man, an African. So what if the boss was black? This was a new life, and she wanted to learn everything. Her Sunday boss, Mr. Anthony, was a courtly, Christian, church-going man, and paid her the only wages she had in her pocket. Viola and Loretta, for all their fancy American ways, wouldn't go out with blacks.

One Friday afternoon she was writing up the credit info on a Guyanese Muslim who worked in an assembly plant when Loretta said that enough was enough and that there was no need for Jasmine to be her father's drudge.

"Is time to have fun," Viola said. "We're going to Ann Arbor."

Jasmine filed the sheet on the Guyanese man who probably now would never get a wife·and got her raincoat. Loretta's boyfriend had a Cadillac parked out front. It was the longest car Jasmine had ever been in and louder than a country bus. Viola's boyfriend got out of the front seat. "Oh, oh, sweet things," he said to Jasmine. "Get in front." He was a talker. She'd learned that much from working on the matrimonial match-ups. She didn't believe him for a second when he said that there were dudes out there dying to ask her out.

Loretta's boyfriend said, "You have eyes I could leap into, girl."

Jasmine knew he was just talking. They sounded like Port-of-Spain boys of three years ago. It didn't surprise her that these Trinidad country boys in Detroit were still behind the times, even of Port-of-Spain. She sat very stiff between the two men, hands on her purse. The Daboo girls laughed in the back seat.

On the highway the girls told her about the reggae night in Ann Arbor. Kevin and the Krazee Islanders. Malcolm's Lovers. All the big reggae groups in the Midwest were converging for the West Indian Students Association fall bash. The ticket didn't come cheap but Jasmine wouldn't let the fellows pay. She wasn't that kind of girl.

The reggae and steel drums brought out the old Jasmine. The rum punch, the dancing, the dreadlocks, the whole combination. She hadn't heard real music since she got to Detroit, where music was supposed to be so famous. The Daboo girls kept turning on rock stuff in the motel lobby whenever their father left the area. She hadn't danced, really *danced*, since she'd left home. It felt so good to dance. She felt hot and sweaty and sexy. The boys at the dance were more than sweet talkers; they moved with assurance and spoke of their futures in America. The bartender gave her two free drinks and said, "Is ready when you are, girl." She ignored him but she felt all hot and good deep inside. She knew Ann Arbor was a special place.

When it was time to pile back into Loretta's boyfriend's Cadillac, she just couldn't face going back to the Plantations Motel and to the Daboos with their accounting books and messy files.

"I don't know what happen, girl," she said to Loretta. "I feel all crazy inside. Maybe is time for me to pursue higher studies in this town."

"This Ann Arbor, girl, they don't just take you off the street. It *cost* like hell."

She spent the night on a bashed-up sofa in the Student Union. She was a well-dressed, respectable girl, and she didn't expect anyone to question her right to sleep on the furniture. Many others were doing the same thing. In the morning, a boy in an army parka showed her the way to the Placement Office. He was a big, blond, clumsy boy, not bad-looking except for the blond eyelashes. He didn't scare her, as did most Americans. She let him buy her a Coke and a hotdog. That evening she had a job with the Moffitts.

Bill Moffitt taught molecular biology and Lara Hatch-Moffitt, his wife, was a performance artist. A performance artist, said Lara, was very different from being an actress, though Jasmine still didn't understand what the difference might be. The Moffitts had a little girl, Muffin, whom Jasmine was to look after, though for the first few months she might have to help out with the housework and the cooking because Lara said she was deep into performance rehearsals. That was all right with her, Jasmine said, maybe a little too quickly. She explained she came from a big family and was used to heavy-duty cooking and cleaning. This wasn't the time to say anything about Ram, the family servant. Americans like the Moffitts wouldn't understand about keeping servants. Ram and she weren't in similar situations. Here mother's helpers, which is what Lara had called her—Americans were good with words to cover their shame—seemed to be as good as anyone.

Lara showed her the room she would have all to herself in the finished basement. There was a big, old TV, not in color like the motel's and a portable typewriter on a desk which Lara said she would find handy when it came time to turn in her term papers. Jasmine didn't say anything about not being a student. She was a student of life, wasn't she? There was a scary moment after they'd discussed what she could expect as salary, which was three times more than anything Mr. Daboo was supposed to pay her but hadn't. She thought Bill Moffitt was going to ask her about her visa or her green card number and social security. But all Bill did was smile and smile at her—he had a wide, pink, baby face—and play with a button on his corduroy jacket. The button would need sewing back on, firmly.

Lara said, "I think I'm going to like you, Jasmine. You have a something about you. A something real special. I'll just bet you've acted, haven't you?" The idea amused her, but she merely smiled and accepted Lara's hug. The interview was over.

Then Bill opened a bottle of Soave and told stories about camping in northern Michigan. He'd been raised there. Jasmine didn't see the point in sleeping in tents; the woods sounded cold and wild and creepy. But she said, "Is exactly what I want to try out come summer, man. Campin and huntin."

Lara asked about Port-of-Spain. There was nothing to tell about her hometown that wouldn't shame her in front of nice white American folk like the Moffitts. The place was shabby, the people were grasping and cheating and lying and life was full of despair and drink and wanting. But by the time she finished, the island sounded romantic. Lara said, "It wouldn't surprise me one bit if you were a writer, Jasmine."

Ann Arbor was a huge small town. She couldn't imagine any kind of school the size of the University of Michigan. She meant to sign up for courses in the spring. Bill brought home a catalogue bigger than the phonebook for all of Trinidad. The university had courses in everything. It would be hard to choose; she'd have to get help from Bill. He wasn't like a professor, not the ones back home where even high school teachers called themselves professors and acted like little potentates. He wore blue jeans and thick sweaters with holes in the elbows and used phrases like "in vitro" as he watched her curry up fish. Dr. Parveen back home—he called himself "doctor" when everybody knew he didn't have even a Master's degree— was never seen without his cotton jacket which had gotten really ratty at the cuffs and lapel edges. She hadn't learned anything in the two years she'd put into college. She'd learned more from working in the bank for two months than she had at college. It was the assistant manager, Personal Loans Department, Mr. Singh, who had turned her on to the Daboos and to smooth, bargain-priced emigration.

Jasmine liked Lara. Lara was easygoing. She didn't spend the time she had between rehearsals telling Jasmine how to cook and clean American-style. Mrs. Daboo did that in 16B. Mrs. Daboo would barge in with a plate of stale samosas and snoop around giving free advice on how mainstream Americans did things. As if she were dumb or something! As if she couldn't keep her own eyes open and make her mind up for herself. Sunday mornings she had to share the butcher-block workspace in the kitchen with Bill. He made the Sunday brunch from new recipes in *Gourmet* and *Cuisine*. Jasmine hadn't seen a man cook who didn't have to or wasn't getting paid to do it. Things were topsy-turvy in the Moffitt house. Lara went on two- and three-day road trips and Bill stayed home. But even her Daddy, who'd never poured himself a cup of tea, wouldn't put Bill down as a woman. The mornings Bill tried out something complicated, a Cajun shrimp, sausage, and beans dish, for instance, Jasmine skipped church services. The Moffitts didn't go to church, though they seemed to be good Christians. They just didn't talk church talk, which suited her fine.

Two months passed. Jasmine knew she was lucky to have found a small, clean, friendly family like the Moffitts to build her new life around. "Man!" she'd exclaim as she vacuumed the wide-plank wood floors or ironed (Lara wore pure silk or pure cotton). "In this country Jesus givin out good luck only!" By this time they knew she wasn't a student, but they didn't care and said they wouldn't report her. They never asked if she was illegal on top of it.

To savor her new sense of being a happy, lucky person, she would put herself through a series of "what ifs": what if Mr. Singh in Port-of-Spain hadn't turned her on to the Daboos and loaned her two thousand! What if she'd been ugly like the Mintoo girl and the manager hadn't even offered! What if the customs man had unlocked the door of the van! Her Daddy liked to say, "You is a helluva girl, Jasmine."

"Thank you, Jesus," Jasmine said, as she carried on.

Christmas Day the Moffitts treated her just like family. They gave her a red cashmere sweater with a V neck so deep it made her blush. If Lara had worn it, her bosom wouldn't hang out like melons. For the holiday weekend Bill drove her to the Daboos in Detroit. "You work too hard," Bill said to her. "Learn to be more selfish. Come on, throw your weight around." She'd rather not have spent time with the Daboos, but that first afternoon of the interview she'd told Bill and Lara that Mr. Daboo was her mother's first cousin. She had thought it shameful in those days to have no papers, no family, no roots. Now Loretta and Viola in tight, bright pants seemed trashy like girls at Two-Johnny Bissoondath's Bar back home. She was stuck with the story of the Daboos being family. Village bumpkins, ha! She would break out. Soon.

Jasmine had Bill drop her off at the RenCen. The Plantations Motel, in fact, the whole Riverfront area, was too seamy. She'd managed to cut herself off mentally from anything too islandy. She loved her Daddy and Mummy, but she didn't think of them that often anymore. Mummy had expected her to be homesick and come flying right back home. "Is blowin sweat-of-brow money is what you doin, Pa," Mummy had scolded. She loved them, but she'd become her own person. That was something that Lara said: "I am my own person."

The Daboos acted thrilled to see her back. "What you drinkin, Jasmine girl?" Mr. Daboo kept asking. "You drinkin sherry or what?" Pouring her little glasses of sherry instead of rum was a sure sign he thought she had become whitefolk-fancy. The Daboo sisters were very friendly, but Jasmine considered them too wild. Both Loretta and Viola had changed boyfriends. Both were seeing black men they'd danced with in Ann Arbor. Each night at bedtime, Mr. Daboo cried. "In Trinidad we stayin we side, they stayin they side. Here, everything mixed up. Is helluva confusion, no?"

On New Year's Eve the Daboo girls and their black friends went to a dance. Mr. and Mrs. Daboo and Jasmine watched TV for a while. Then Mr. Daboo got out a brooch from his pocket and pinned it on Jasmine's red sweater. It was a Christmasy brooch, a miniature sleigh loaded down with snowed-on mistletoe. Before she could pull away, he kissed her on the lips. "Good luck for the New Year!" he said. She lifted her head and saw tears. "Is year for dreams comin true."

Jasmine started to cry, too. There was nothing wrong, but Mr. Daboo, Mrs. Daboo, she, everybody was crying.

What for? This is where she wanted to be. She'd spent some damned uncomfortable times with the assistant manager to get approval for her loan. She thought of Daddy. He would be playing poker and fanning himself with a magazine. Her married sisters would be rolling out the dough for stacks and stacks of roti, and Mummy would be steamed purple from stirring the big pot of goat curry on the stove. She missed them. But. It felt strange to think of anyone celebrating New Year's Eve in summery clothes.

In March Lara and her performing group went on the road. Jasmine knew that the group didn't work from scripts. The group didn't use a stage, either; instead, it took over supermarkets, senior citizens' centers, and school halls, without notice. Jasmine didn't understand the performance world. But she was glad that Lara said, "I'm not going to lay a guilt trip on myself. Muffie's in super hands," before she left.

Muffie didn't need much looking after. She played Trivial Pursuit all day, usually pretending to be two persons, sometimes Jasmine, whose accent she could imitate. Since Jasmine didn't know any of the answers, she couldn't help. Muffie was a quiet, precocious child with see-through blue eyes like her dad's, and red braids. In the early evenings Jasmine cooked supper, something special she hadn't forgotten from her island days. After supper she and Muffie watched some TV, and Bill read. When Muffie went to bed, Bill and she sat together for a bit with their glasses of Soave. Bill, Muffie, and she were a family, almost.

Down in her basement room that late, dark winter, she had trouble sleeping. She wanted to stay awake and think of Bill. Even when she fell asleep it didn't feel like sleep because Bill came barging into her dreams in his funny, loose-jointed, clumsy way. It was mad to think of him all the time, and stupid and sinful; but she couldn't help it. Whenever she put back a book he'd taken off the shelf to read or whenever she put his clothes through the washer and dryer, she felt sick in a giddy, wonderful way. When Lara came back things would get back to normal. Meantime she wanted the performance group miles away.

Lara called in at least twice a week. She said things like, "We've finally obliterated the margin between realspace and performancespace." Jasmine filled her in on Muffie's doings and the mail. Bill always closed with, "I love you. We miss you, hon."

One night after Lara had called—she was in Lincoln, Nebraska—Bill said to Jasmine, "Let's dance."

She hadn't danced since the reggae night she'd had too many rum punches. Her toes began to throb and clench. She untied her apron and the fraying, knotted-up laces of her running shoes.

Bill went around the downstairs rooms turning down lights. "We need atmosphere," he said. He got a small, tidy fire going in the living room grate and pulled the Turkish scatter rug closer to it. Lara didn't like anybody walking on the Turkish rug, but Bill meant to have his way. The hissing logs, the plants in the dimmed light, the thick patterned rug: everything was changed. This wasn't the room she cleaned every day.

He stood close to her. She smoothed her skirt down with both hands.

"I want you to choose the record," he said.

"I don't know your music."

She brought her hand high to his face. His skin was baby smooth.

"I want *you* to pick," he said. "You are your own person now."

"You got island music?"

He laughed, "What do you think?" The stereo was in a cabinet with albums packed tight alphabetically into the bottom three shelves. "Calypso has not been a force in my life."

She couldn't help laughing. "Calypso? Oh, man." She pulled dust jackets out at random. Lara's records. The Flying Lizards. The Violent Fems. There was so much still to pick up on!

"This one," she said, finally

He took the record out of her hand. "God! he laughed. "Lara must have found this in a garage sale!" He laid the old record on the turntable. It was "Music for Lovers," something the nuns had taught her to foxtrot to way back in Port-of-Spain.

They danced so close that she could feel his heart heaving and crashing against her head. She liked it, she liked it very much. She didn't care what happened.

"Come on," Bill whispered. "If it feels right, do it." He began to take her clothes off.

"Don't, Bill," she pleaded.

"Come on, baby," he whispered again. "You're a blossom, a flower."

He took off his fisherman's knit pullover, the corduroy pants, the blue shorts. She kept pace. She'd never had such an effect on a man. He nearly flung his socks and Adidas into the fire. "You feel so good," he said. "You smell so good. You're really something, flower of Trinidad."

"Flower of Ann Arbor," she said, "not Trinidad."

She felt so good she was dizzy. She'd never felt this good on the island where men did this all the time, and girls went along with it always for favors. You couldn't feel really good in a nothing place. She was thinking this as they made love on the Turkish carpet in front of the fire: she was a bright, pretty girl with no visa, no papers, and no birth certificate. No nothing other than what she wanted to invent and tell. She was a girl rushing wildly into the future.

His hand moved up her throat and forced her lips apart and it felt so good, so right, that she forgot all the dreariness of her new life and gave herself up to it.

DANNY'S
GIRLS

I WAS thirteen when Danny Sahib moved into our building in Flushing. That was his street name, but my Aunt Lini still called him Dinesh, the name he'd landed with. He was about twenty, a Dogra boy from Simla with slicked-back hair and coppery skin. If he'd worked on his body language, he could have passed for Mexican, which might have been useful. Hispanics are taken more seriously, in certain lines of business, than Indians. But I don't want to give the wrong impression about Danny. He wasn't an enforcer, he was a charmer. No one was afraid of him; he was a merchant of opportunity. I got to know him because he was always into ghetto scams that needed junior high boys like me to pull them off.

He didn't have parents, at least none that he talked about, and he boasted he'd been on his own since he was six. I admired that, I wished I could escape my family, such as it was. My parents had been bounced from Uganda by Idi Amin, and then barred from England by some parliamentary trickery. Mother's sister—Aunt Lini—sponsored us in the States. I don't remember Africa at all, but my father could never forget that we'd once had servants and two Mercedes-Benzes. He sat around Lini's house moaning about the good old days and grumbling about how hard life in America was until finally the women organized a coup and chucked him out. My mother sold papers in the subway kiosks, twelve hours a day, seven days a week. Last I heard, my father was living with a Trinidad woman in Philadelphia, but we haven't seen him or talked about him for years. So in Danny's mind I was an orphan, like him.

He wasn't into the big-money stuff like drugs. He was a hustler, nothing more. He used to boast that he knew some guys, Nepalese and Pakistanis, who could supply him with anything—but we figured that was just talk. He started out with bets and scalping tickets for Lata Mangeshkar or Mithun Chakravorty concerts at Madison Square Garden. Later he fixed beauty contests and then discovered the marriage racket.

Danny took out ads in papers in India promising "guaranteed Permanent Resident status in the U.S." to grooms willing to proxy-marry American girls of Indian origin. He arranged quite a few. The brides and grooms didn't have to live with each other, or even meet or see each other. Sometimes the "brides" were smooth-skinned boys from the neighborhood. He used to audition his brides in our apartment and coach them—especially the boys—on keeping their faces low, their saris high, and their arms as glazed and smooth as caramel. The immigration inspectors never suspected a thing. I never understood why young men would pay a lot of money—I think the going rate was fifty thousand rupees—to come here. Maybe if I remembered the old country I might feel different. I've never even visited India.

Flushing was full of greedy women. I never met one who would turn down gold or a fling with the money market. The streets were lousy with gold merchants, more gold emporia than pizza parlors. Melt down the hoarded gold of Jackson Heights and you could plate the Queensboro Bridge. My first job for Danny Sahib was to approach the daughters in my building for bride volunteers and a fifty buck fee, and then with my sweet, innocent face, sign a hundred dollar contract with their mothers.

Then Danny Sahib saw he was thinking small. The real money wasn't in rupees and bringing poor saps over. It was in selling docile Indian girls to hard-up Americans for real bucks. An Old World wife who knew her place and would breed like crazy was worth at least twenty thousand dollars. To sweeten the deal and get some good-looking girls for his catalogues, Danny promised to send part of the fee back to India. No one in India could even imagine *getting* money for the curse of having a daughter. So he expanded his marriage business to include mail-order brides, and he offered my smart Aunt Lini a partnership. My job was to put up posters in the laundromats and pass out flyers on the subways.

Aunt Lini was a shrewd businesswoman, a widow who'd built my uncle's small-time investor service for cautious Gujarati gentlemen into a full-scale loan-sharking operation that financed half the Indian-owned taxi medallions in Queens. Her rates were simple: double the prime, no questions asked. Triple the prime if she smelled a risk, which she usually did. She ran it out of her kitchen with a phone next to the stove. She could turn a thousand dollars while frying up a *bhaji*.

Aunt Lini's role was to warehouse the merchandise, as she called the girls, that couldn't be delivered to its American destination (most of those American fiancés had faces a fly wouldn't buzz). Aunt Lini had spare rooms she could turn into an informal S.R.O. hotel. She called the rooms her "pet shop" and she thought of the girls as puppies in the window. In addition to the flat rate that Danny paid her, she billed the women separately for bringing gentlemen guests, or shoppers, into the room. This encouraged a prompt turnover. The girls found it profitable to make an expeditious decision.

The summer I was fifteen, Aunt Lini had a paying guest, a Nepalese, a real looker. Her skin was white as whole milk, not the color of tree bark I was accustomed to. Her lips were a peachy orange and she had high Nepalese cheekbones. She called herself "Rosie" in the mail-order catalogue and listed her age as sixteen. Danny wanted all his girls to be sixteen and most of them had names like Rosie and Dolly. I suppose when things didn't work out between her and her contract "fiancé" she saw no reason to go back to her real name. Or especially, back to some tubercular hut in Katmandu. Her parents certainly wouldn't take her back. They figured she was married and doing time in Toledo with a dude named Duane.

Rosie liked to have me around. In the middle of a sizzling afternoon she would send me to Mr. Chin's store for a pack of Kents, or to Ranjit's liquor store for gin. She was a good tipper, or maybe she couldn't admit to me that she couldn't add. The money came from Danny, part of her "dowry" that he didn't send back to Nepal. I knew she couldn't read or write, not even in her own language. That didn't bother me—guaranteed illiteracy is a big selling point in the mail-order bride racket—and there was nothing abject about her. I'd have to say she was a proud woman. The other girls Danny brought over were already broken in spirit; they'd marry just about any freak Danny brought around. Not Rosie—she'd throw some of them out, and threaten others with a cobra she said she kept in her suitcase if they even thought of touching her. After most of my errands, she'd ask me to sit on the bed and light me a cigarette and pour me a weak drink. I'd fan her for a while with the newspaper.

"What are you going to be when you finish school?" she'd ask me and blow rings, like kisses, that wobbled to my face and broke gently across it. I didn't know anyone who blew smoke rings. I thought they had gone out with black-and-white films. I became a staunch admirer of Nepal.

What I wanted to be in those days was someone important, which meant a freedom like Danny's but without the scams. Respectable freedom in the bigger world of America, that's what I wanted. Growing up in Queens gives a boy ambitions. But I didn't disclose them. I said to Rosie what my Ma always said when other Indians dropped by. I said I would be going to Columbia University to the Engineering School. It was a story

Ma believed because she'd told it so often, though I knew better. Only the Indian doctors' kids from New Jersey and Long Island went to Columbia. Out in Flushing we got a different message. Indian boys were placed on earth to become accountants and engineers. Even old *Idi Amin* was placed on earth to force Indians to come to America to become accountants and engineers. I went through high school scared, wondering what there was in my future if I hated numbers. I wondered if Pace and Adelphi had engineering. I didn't want to turn out like my Aunt Lini, a ghetto moneylender, and I didn't want to suffer like my mother, and I hated my father with a passion. No wonder Danny's world seemed so exciting. My mother was knocking herself out at a kiosk in Port Authority, earning the minimum wage from a guy who convinced her he was doing her a big favor, all for my mythical Columbia tuition. Lini told me that in America grades didn't count; it was all in the test scores. She bought me the SAT workbooks and told me to memorize the answers.

"Smashing," Rosie would say, and other times, "Jolly good," showing that even in the Himalayan foothills, the sun hadn't yet set on the British Empire.

Some afternoons Rosie would be doubled over in bed with leg pains. I know now she'd had rickets as a kid and spent her childhood swaying under hundred pound sacks of rice piled on her head. By thirty she'd be hobbling around like an old football player with blown knees. But at sixteen or whatever, she still had great, hard, though slightly bent legs, and she'd hike her velour dressing gown so I could tightly crisscross her legs and part of her thighs with pink satin hair ribbons. It was a home remedy, she said, it stopped circulation. I couldn't picture her in that home, Nepal. She was like a queen ("The Queen of Queens," I used to joke) to me that year. Even India, where both my parents were born, was a mystery.

Curing Rosie's leg pains led to some strong emotions, and soon I wanted to beat on the gentlemen callers who came, carrying cheap boxes of candy and looking her over like a slave girl on the auction block. She'd tell me about it, nonchalantly, making it funny. She'd catalogue each of their faults, imitate their voices. They'd try to get a peek under the covers or even under the clothing, and Danny would be there to cool things down. I wasn't allowed to help, but by then I would have killed for her.

I was no stranger to the miseries of unrequited love. Rosie was the unavailable love in the room upstairs who talked to me unblushingly of sex and made the whole transaction seem base and grubby and funny. In my Saturday morning Gujarati class, on the other hand, there was a girl from Syosset who called herself "Pammy Patel," a genuine Hindu-American Princess of the sort I had never seen before, whose skin and voice and eyes were as soft as clouds. She wore expensive dresses and you could tell she'd spent hours making herself up just for the Gujarati classes in the Hindu Temple. Her father was a major surgeon, and he and Pammy's brothers would stand outside the class to protect her from any contact with boys like me. They would watch us filing out of the classroom, looking us up and down and smirking the way Danny's catalogue brides were looked at by their American buyers.

I found the whole situation achingly romantic. In the Hindi films I'd see every Sunday, the hero was always a common man with a noble heart, in love with an unattainable beauty. Then she'd be kidnapped and he'd have to save her. Caste and class would be overcome and marriage would follow. To that background, I added a certain American equality. I grew up hating rich people, especially rich Indian immigrants who didn't have the problems of Uganda and a useless father, but otherwise were no better than I. I never gave them the deference that Aunt Lini and my mother did.

With all that behind me, I had assumed that real love *had* to be cheerless. I had assumed I wouldn't find a girl worth marrying, not that girls like Pammy could make me happy. Rosie was the kind of girl who could make me happy, but even I knew she was not the kind of girl I could marry. It was confusing.

Thoughts of Rosie made me want to slash the throats of rivals. Thoughts of Pammy made me want to wipe out her whole family.

One very hot afternoon Rosie, as usual, leaned her elbows on the windowsill and shouted to me to fetch a six-pack of tonic and a lemon. I'd been sitting on the stoop, getting new tips from Danny on scalping for an upcoming dance recital—a big one, Lincoln Center—but I leaped to attention and shook the change in my pockets to make sure I had enough for Mr. Chin. Rosie kept records of her debts, and she'd pay them off, she said, just as soon as Danny arranged a green card to make her legit. She intended to make it here without getting married. She exaggerated Danny's power. To her, he was some kind of local bigwig who could pull off anything. None of Danny's girls had tried breaking a contract before, and I wondered if she'd actually taken it up with him.

Danny pushed me back so hard I scraped my knee on the stoop. "You put up the posters," he said. After taping them up, I was to circulate on the subway and press the pictures on every lonely guy I saw. "I'll take care of Rosie. You report back tomorrow."

"After I get her tonic and a lemon," I said.

It was the only time I ever saw the grown-up orphan in Danny, the survivor. If he'd had a knife or a gun on him, he might have used it. "I give the orders," he said, " you follow." Until that moment, I'd always had the implicit sense that Danny and I were partners in some exciting enterprise, that together we were putting something over on India, on Flushing, and even on America.

Then he smiled, but it wasn't Danny's radiant, conspiratorial, arm-on-the-shoulder smile that used to warm my day. "You're making her fat," he said. "You're making her drunk. You probably want to diddle her yourself, don't you? Fifteen years old and never been out of your Auntie's house and you want a real woman like Rosie. But she thinks you're her errand boy and you just love being her smiley little *chokra-boy*, don't you?" Then the smile froze on his lips, and if he'd ever looked Mexican, this was the time. Then he said something in Hindi that I barely understood, and he laughed as he watched me repeat it, slowly. Something about eunuchs not knowing their place. "Don't ever go up there again, *hijra*-boy."

I was starting to take care of Danny's errands quickly and sloppily as always, and then, at the top of the subway stairs, I stopped. I'd never really thought what a strange, pimpish thing I was doing, putting up pictures of Danny's girls, or standing at the top of the subway stairs and passing them out to any lonely-looking American I saw—what kind of joke was this? How dare he do this, I thought, how dare he make me a part of this? I couldn't move. I had two hundred sheets of yellow paper in my hands, descriptions of Rosie and half a dozen others like her, and instead of passing them out, I threw them over my head and let them settle on the street and sidewalk and filter down the paper-strewn, garbage-littered steps of the subway. How dare he call me *hijra*, eunuch?

I got back to Aunt Lini's within the hour. She was in her kitchen charring an eggplant. " I'm making a special *bharta* for you," she said, clapping a hand over the receiver. She was putting the screws on some poor Sikh, judging from the stream of coarse Punjabi I heard as I tore through the kitchen. She shouted after me, "Your Ma'll be working late tonight." More guilt, more Columbia, more engineering.

I didn't thank Aunt Lini for being so thoughtful, and I didn't complain about Ma not being home for me. I was in a towering rage with Rosie and with everyone who ever slobbered over her picture.

"Take your shoes off in the hall," Lini shouted. "You know the rules."

I was in the mood to break rules. For the first time I could remember, I wasn't afraid of Danny Sahib. I wanted to liberate Rosie, and myself. From the hall stand I grabbed the biggest, sturdiest, wood-handled umbrella—gentlemen callers were always leaving behind souvenirs—and in my greasy high-tops I clumped up the stairs two at a time and kicked open the door to Rosie's room.

Rosie lay in bed, smoking. She'd propped a new fan on her pillow, near her face. She sipped her gin and lime. *So,* I thought in my fit of mad jealousy, he's bought her a fan. And now suddenly she likes limes. Damn him, *damn* him. She won't want me and my newspapers, she won't want my lemons. I wouldn't have cared if Danny and half the bachelors in Queens were huddled around that bed. I was so pumped up with the enormity of love that I beat the mattress in the absence of rivals. Whack! Whack! Whack! went the stolen umbrella, and Rosie bent her legs delicately to get them out of the way. The fan teetered off the pillow and lay there beside her on the wilted, flopping bed, blowing hot air at the ceiling. She held her drink up tight against her nose and lips and stared at me around the glass.

"So, you want me, do you?" she said.

Slowly, she moved the flimsy little fan, then let it drop. I knelt on the floor with my head on the pillow that had pressed into her body, smelling flowers I would never see in Flushing and feeling the tug on my shoulder that meant I should come up to bed and for the first time I felt my life was going to be A-Okay.

BURIED
LIVES

ONE March midafternoon in Trincomalee, Sri Lanka, Mr. N. K. S. Venkatesan, a forty-nine-year-old schoolteacher who should have been inside a St. Joseph's Collegiate classroom explicating Arnold's "The Buried Life" found himself instead at a barricaded intersection, axe in hand and shouting rude slogans at a truckload of soldiers.

Mr. Venkatesan was not a political man. In his neighborhood he was the only householder who hadn't contributed, not even a rupee, to the Tamil Boys' Sporting Association, which everyone knew wasn't a cricket club so much as a recruiting center for the Liberation Tigers. And at St. Joe's, he hadn't signed the staff petition abhorring the arrest at a peaceful anti-Buddhist demonstration of Dr. Pillai, the mathematics teacher. Venkatesan had rather enjoyed talking about fractals with Dr. Pillai, but he disapproved of men with family responsibilities sticking their heads between billy clubs as though they were still fighting the British for independence.

Fractals claimed to predict, mathematically, chaos and apparent randomness. Such an endeavor, if possible, struck Mr. Venkatesan as a virtually holy quest, closer to the spirit of religion than of science. What had once been Ceylon was now Sri Lanka.

Mr. Venkatesan, like Dr. Pillai, had a large family to look after: he had parents, one set of grandparents, an aunt who hadn't been quite right in the head since four of her five boys had signed up with the Tigers, and three much younger, unmarried sisters. They lived with him in a three-room flat above a variety store. It was to protect his youngest sister (a large, docile girl who, before she got herself mixed up with the Sporting Association, used to embroider napkin-and-table-cloth sets and sell them to a middleman for export to fancy shops in Canada) that he was marching that afternoon with two hundred baby-faced protesters.

Axe under arm—he held the weapon as he might an umbrella—Mr. Venkatesan and his sister and a frail boy with a bushy moustache on whom his sister appeared to have a crush, drifted past looted stores and charred vehicles. In the center of the intersection, a middle-aged leader in camouflage fatigues and a black beret stood on the roof of a van without tires, and was about to set fire to the national flag with what looked to Mr. Venkatesan very much like a Zippo lighter.

"Sir, you have to get in the mood," said his sister's boyfriend. The moustache entirely covered his mouth. Mr. Venkatesan had the uncanny sensation of being addressed by a thatch of undulating bristles. "You have to let yourself go, sir."

This wasn't advice; this was admonition. Around Mr. Venkatesan swirled dozens of hyperkinetic boys in white shirts, holding bricks. Fat girls in summer frocks held placards aloft. His sister sucked on an ice cream bar. Every protester seemed to twinkle with fun. He didn't know how to have fun, that was the trouble. Even as an adolescent he'd battened down all passion; while other students had slipped love notes into expectant palms, he'd studied, he'd passed exams. Dutifulness had turned him into a pariah.

"Don't think you chaps invented civil disobedience!"

He lectured the boyfriend on how his generation—meaning that technically, he'd been alive though hardly self-conscious—had cowed the British Empire. The truth was that the one time the police had raided the Venkatesans' flat—he'd been four, but he'd been taught anti-British phrases like "the salt march" and "*satyagraha*" by a cousin ten years older—he had saluted the superintendant smartly even as constables squeezed his cousin's wrists into handcuffs. That cousin was now in San Jose, California, minting lakhs and lakhs of dollars in computer software.

The boyfriend, still smiling awkwardly, moved away from Mr. Venkatesan's sister. His buddies, Tigers in berets, were clustered around a vendor of spicy fritters.

"Wait!" the sister pleaded, her face puffy with held-back tears.

"What do you see in that callow, good-for-nothing bloke?" Mr. Venkatesan asked.

"Please, please leave me alone," his sister screamed. "Please let me do what I want."

What if *he* were to do what he wanted! Twenty years ago when he'd had the chance, he should have applied for a Commonwealth Scholarship. He should have immured himself in a leafy dormitory in Oxford. Now it was too late. He'd have studied law. Maybe he'd have married an English girl and loitered abroad. But both parents had died, his sisters were mere toddlers, and he was obliged to take the lowest, meanest teaching job in the city.

"I want to die," his sister sobbed beside him.

"Shut up, you foolish girl."

The ferocity of her passion for the worthless boy, who was, just then, biting into a greasy potato fritter, shocked him. He had patronized her when she had been a plain, pliant girl squinting at embroidered birds and flowers. But now something harsh and womanly seemed to be happening inside her.

"Forget those chaps. They're nothing but troublemakers." To impress her, he tapped a foot to the beat of a slogan bellowing out of loudspeakers.

Though soldiers were starting to hustle demonstrators into double-parked paddy wagons, the intersection had taken on the gaudiness of a village fair. A white-haired vendor darted from police jeep to jeep hawking peanuts in paper cones. Boys who had drunk too much tea or soda relieved themselves freely into poster-clogged gutters. A dozen feet up the road a housewife with a baby on her hip lobbed stones into storefronts. A band of beggars staggered out of an electronics store with a radio and a television. No reason not to get in the mood.

"Blood for blood," he shouted, timidly at first. "Blood begets blood."

"Begets?" the man beside him asked. "What's that supposed to mean?" In his plastic sandals and cheap drawstring pajamas, the man looked like a coolie or laborer.

He turned to his sister for commiseration. What could she expect him to have in common with a mob of uneducated men like that? But she'd left him behind. He saw her, crouched for flight like a giant ornament on the hood of an old-fashioned car, the March wind stiffly splaying her sari and long hair behind her.

"Get down from that car!" he cried. But the crowd, swirling, separated him from her. He felt powerless; he could no longer watch over her, keep her out of the reach of night sticks. From on top of the hood she taunted policemen, and not just policemen but everybody— shopgirls and beggars and ochre-robed monks— as though she wasn't just a girl with a crush on a Tiger but a monster out of one's most splenetic nightmares.

Months later, in a boardinghouse in Hamburg, Mr. Venkatesan couldn't help thinking about the flock of young monks pressed together behind a police barricade that eventful afternoon. He owed his freedom to the monks because, in spite of their tonsure scars and their vows of stoicism, that afternoon they'd behaved like any other hot-headed Sri Lankan adolescents. If the monks hadn't chased his sister and knocked her off the pale blue hood of the car, Mr. Venkatesan would have stayed on in Sri Lanka, in Trinco, in St. Joe's teaching the same poems year after year, a permanent prisoner.

What the monks did was unforgivable. Robes plucked knee-high and celibate lips plumped up in vengeful chant, they pulled a girl by the hair, and they slapped and spat and kicked with vigor worthy of newly initiated Tigers.

It could have been another girl, somebody else's younger sister. Without thinking, Mr. Venkatesan rotated a shoulder, swung an arm, readied his mind to inflict serious harm.

It should never have happened. The axe looped clumsily over the heads of demonstrators and policemen and fell, like a captured kite, into the hands of a Home Guards officer. There was blood, thick and purplish, spreading in jagged stains on the man's white uniform. The crowd wheeled violently. The drivers of paddy wagons laid panicky fingers on their horns. Veils of tear gas blinded enemies and friends. Mr. Venkatesan, crying and choking, ducked into a store and listened to the thwack of batons. When his vision eased, he staggered, still on automatic pilot, down side streets and broke through garden hedges all the way to St. Joseph's unguarded backdoor.

In the men's room off the Teacher's Common Room he held his face, hot with guilt, under a rusty, hissing faucet until Father van der Haagen, the Latin and Scriptures teacher, came out of a stall.

"You don't look too well. Sleepless night, eh?" the Jesuit joked. "You need to get married, Venkatesan. Bad habits can't always satisfy you."

Mr. Venkatesan laughed dutifully. All of Father van der Haagen's jokes had to do with masturbation. He didn't say anything about having deserted his sister. He didn't say anything about having maimed, maybe murdered, a Home Guards officer. "Who can afford a wife on what the school pays?" he joked back. Then he hurried off to his classroom.

Though he was over a half-hour late, his students were still seated meekly at their desks.

"Good afternoon, sir." Boys in monogrammed shirts and rice-starched shorts shuffled to standing positions.

"Sit!" the schoolmaster commanded. Without taking his eyes

off the students, he opened his desk and let his hand locate *A Treasury of the Most Dulcet Verses Written in the English Language*, which he had helped the headmaster to edit though only the headmaster's name appeared on the book.

Matthew Arnold was Venkatesan's favorite poet. Mr. Venkatesan had talked the Head into including four Arnold poems. The verses picked by the Head hadn't been "dulcet" at all, and one hundred and three pages of the total of one hundred and seventy-four had been given over to upstart Trinco versifiers' martial ballads.

Mr. Venkatesan would have nursed a greater bitterness against the Head if the man hadn't vanished, mysteriously, soon after their acrimonious coediting job.

One winter Friday the headmaster had set out for his nightly after-dinner walk, and he hadn't come back. The Common Room gossip was that he had been kidnapped by a paramilitary group. But Miss Philomena, the female teacher who was by tradition permitted the use of the Head's private bathroom, claimed the man had drowned in the Atlantic Ocean trying to sneak into Canada in a boat that ferried, for a wicked fee, illegal aliens. Stashed in the bathroom's air vent (through which sparrows sometimes flew in and bothered her), she'd spotted, she said, an oilcloth pouch stuffed with foreign cash and fake passports.

In the Teacher's Common Room, where Miss Philomena was not popular, her story was discounted. But at the Pillais's home, the men teachers had gotten together and toasted the Head with hoarded bottles of whiskey and sung many rounds of "For He's a Jolly Good Fellow," sometimes substituting "smart" for "good." By the time Mr. Venkatesan had been dropped home by Father van der Haagen, who owned a motorcycle, night had bleached itself into rainy dawn. It had been the only all-nighter of Mr. Venkatesan's life and the only time he might have been accused of drunkenness.

The memory of how good the rain had felt came back to him

now as he glanced through the first stanza of the assigned Arnold poem. What was the function of poetry if not to improve the petty, cautious minds of evasive children? What was the duty of the teacher if not to inspire?

He cleared his throat, and began to read aloud in a voice trained in elocution.

> Light flows our war of mocking words, and yet,
> Behold, with tears mine eyes are wet!
> I feel a nameless sadness o'er me roll.
> Yes, yes, we know that we can jest,
> We know, we know that we can smile!
> But there's a something in this breast,
> To which thy light words bring no rest,
> And thy gay smiles no anodyne.
> Give me thy hand, and hush awhile,
> And turn those limpid eyes on mine,
> And let me read there, love! thy inmost soul.

"Sir," a plump boy in the front row whispered as Venkatesan finally stopped for breath.

"What is it now?" snapped Venkatesan. In his new mood Arnold had touched him with fresh intensity, and he hated the boy for deflating illusion. "If you are wanting to know a synonym for 'anodyne,' then look it up in the *Oxford Dictionary*. You are a lazy donkey wanting me to feed you with a silver spoon. All of you, you are all lazy donkeys."

"No, sir." The boy persisted in spoiling the mood.

It was then that Venkatesan took in the boy's sweaty face and hair. Even the eyes were fat and sweaty.

"Behold, sir," the boy said. He dabbed his eyelids with the limp tip of his school tie. "Mine eyes, too, are wet."

"You are a silly donkey," Venkatesan yelled. "You are a beast of burden. You deserve the abuse that you get. It is you emotional types who are selling this country down the river."

The class snickered, unsure what Mr. Venkatesan wanted of them. The boy let go of his tie and wept openly. Mr. Venkatesan hated himself. Here was a kindred soul, a fellow lover of Matthew Arnold, and what had he done other than indulge in gratuitous cruelty? He blamed the times. He blamed Sri Lanka.

It was as much this classroom incident as the fear of arrest for his part in what turned out to be an out-of-control demonstration that made Mr. Venkatesan look into emigrating. At first, he explored legal channels. He wasted a month's salary bribing arrogant junior-level clerks in four consulates—he was willing to settle almost anywhere except in the Gulf Emirates—but every country he could see himself being happy and fulfilled in turned him down.

So all through the summer he consoled himself with reading novels. Adventure stories in which fearless young Britons—sailors, soldiers, missionaries—whacked wildernesses into submission. From lending libraries in the city, he checked out books that were so old that they had to be trussed with twine. On the flyleaf of each book, in fading ink, was an inscription by a dead or retired British tea planter. Like the blond heroes of the novels, the colonials must have come to Ceylon chasing dreams of perfect futures. He, too, must sail dark, stormy oceans.

In August, at the close of a staff meeting, Miss Philomena announced coyly that she was leaving the island. A friend in Kalamazoo, Michigan, had agreed to sponsor her as a "domestic."

"It is a ploy only, man," Miss Philomena explained. "In the autumn, I am signing up for post-graduate studies in a prestigious educational institution."

"You are cleaning toilets and whatnot just like a servant girl? Is the meaning of 'domestic' not the same as 'servant'?"

Mr. Venkatesan joined the others in teasing Miss Philomena, but late that night he wrote away to eight American universities for applications. He took great care with the cover letters, which always began with "Dear Respected Sir" and ended with "Humbly but eagerly awaiting your response." He tried to put down in the allotted blanks what it felt like to be born so heartbreakingly far from New York or London. *On this small dead-end island, I feel I am a shadow-man, a nothing. I feel I'm a stranger in my own room. What consoles me is reading. I sink my teeth into fiction by great Englishmen such as G. A. Henty and A. E. W. Mason. I live my life through their imagined lives. And when I put their works down at dawn I ask myself, Hath not a Tamil eyes, heart, ears, nose, throat, to adapt the words of the greatest Briton. Yes, I am a Tamil. If you prick me, do I not bleed? If you tickle me, do I not laugh? Then, if I dream, will you not give me a chance, respected Sir, as only you can?*

In a second paragraph he politely but firmly indicated the size of scholarship he would require, and indicated the size of apartment he (and his sisters) would require. He preferred close proximity to campus, since he did not intend to drive.

But sometime in late April, the school's porter brought him, rubber-banded together, eight letters of rejection.

"I am worthless," Mr. Venkatesan moaned in front of the porter. "I am a donkey."

The porter offered him aspirins. "You are unwell, sahib."

The schoolteacher swallowed the tablets, but as soon as the servant left, he snatched a confiscated Zippo lighter from his desk and burned the rejections.

When he got home, his sister's suitor was on the balcony, painting placards, and though he meant to say nothing to the youth, meant to admit no flaw, no defeat, his body betrayed him with shudders and moans.

"Racism!" the youth spat as he painted over a spelling error that, even in his grief, Mr. Venkatesan couldn't help pointing out. "Racism is what's slamming the door in your face, man! You got to improvise your weapons!"

Perhaps the boy was not a totally unworthy suitor. He let the exclamations play in his head, and soon the rejections, and the anxiety that he might be stuck on the futureless island fired him up instead of depressing him. Most nights he lay in bed fully dressed—the police always raided at dawn—and thought up a hundred illegal but feasible ways to outwit immigration officials.

The least wild schemes he talked over with Father van der Haagen. Long ago and in another country, Father van der Haagen had surely given in to similar seductions. The Jesuit usually hooted, "So you want to rot in a freezing, foreign jail? You want your lovely sisters to walk the streets and come to harm?" But, always, the expatriate ended these chats with his boyhood memories of skating on frozen Belgian rivers and ponds. Mr. Venkatesan felt he could visualize snow, but not a whole river so iced up that it was as solid as a grand trunk highway. In his dreams, the Tamil schoolteacher crisscrossed national boundaries on skates that felt as soft and comforting as cushions.

In August his sister's suitor got himself stupidly involved in a prison break. The sister came to Mr. Venkatesan weeping. She had stuffed clothes and her sewing basket into a camouflage satchel. She was going into the northern hills, she said. The Tigers could count on the tea pickers.

"No way," Mr. Venkatesan exploded. When he was safely in America's heartland, with his own wife and car and all accoutrements of New World hearth and home, he wanted to think of his Trinco family (to whom he meant to remit generous monthly sums) as being happy under one roof, too. "You are not going to live with hooligan types in jungles."

"If you lock me in my room, I'll call the police. I'll tell them who threw the axe at the rally."

"Is that what they teach you in guerrilla camps? To turn on your family?" he demanded.

The sister wept loudly into her sari. It was a pretty lilac sari, and he remembered having bought it for her seventeenth birthday. On her feet were fragile lilac slippers. He couldn't picture her scrambling up terraced slopes of tea estates in that pretty get-up. "Nobody has to teach me," she retorted.

In her lilac sari, and with the white fragrant flower wreath in her hair, she didn't look like a blackmailer. It was the times. She, her boyfriend, he himself, were all fate's victims.

He gave in. He made her promise, though, that in the hills she would marry her suitor. She touched his feet with her forehead in the traditional farewell. He heard a scooter start up below. So the guerrilla had been waiting. She'd meant to leave home, with or without his permission. She'd freed herself of family duties and bonds.

Above the motor scooter's sputter, the grateful boyfriend shouted, "Sir, I will put you in touch with a man. Listen to him and he will deliver you." Then the dust cloud of destiny swallowed up the guerrilla bride-to-be and groom.

The go-between turned out to be a clubfooted and cauliflower-eared middle-aged man. The combination of deformities, no doubt congenital, had nevertheless earned him a reputation for ferocity and an indifference to inflicted suffering. He appeared on the front porch early one Saturday afternoon. He didn't come straight to the point. For the first half-hour he said very little and concentrated instead on the sweet almond-stuffed turnovers that the Venkatesan family had shaped and fried all day for a religious festival they'd be attending later that afternoon.

"You have, perhaps, some news for me?" Mr. Venkatesan asked shyly as he watched the man help himself to a chilled glass of mango fool. "Some important information, no?"

"Excuse me, sir," the man protested. "I know that you are a teacher and that therefore you are in the business of improving the mind of man. But forthrightness is not always a virtue. Especially in these troubled times."

The man's furtiveness was infectious, and Mr. Venkatesan, without thinking, thinned his voice to a hiss. "You are going over my options with me, no?"

"Options!" the man sneered. Then he took out a foreign-looking newspaper from a shopping bag. On a back page of the paper was a picture of three dour sahibs fishing for lobster. "You get my meaning, sir? They have beautiful coves in Nova Scotia. They have beautiful people in the Canadian Maritimes."

On cushiony skates and with clean, cool winds buoying him from behind, Mr. Venkatesan glided all the way into Halifax, dodging posses of border police. He married a girl with red, dimpled cheeks, and all winter she made love to him under a goose-down quilt. Summers he set lobster traps. Editors of quarterlies begged to see his poetry.

"Beautiful people, Canadians," he agreed.

"Not like the damn Americans!" The go-between masticated sternly. "They are sending over soldiers of fortune and suchlike to crush us."

Mr. Venkatesan, wise in ways of middlemen, asked, "This means you're not having a pipeline to America?"

The agent dipped into a bowl of stale fried banana chips. "No matter. The time has come for me to leave."

The next day, Sunday, the man came back to find out how much Mr. Venkatesan might be willing to pay for a fake passport / airline tickets / safe houses en route package deal. Mr. Venkatesan named a figure.

"So you are not really anxious to exit?" the man said.

Mr. Venkatesan revised his figure. He revised the figure three more times before the go-between would do anything more human than sigh at him.

He was being taken by a mean, mocking man who preyed on others' dreams. He was allowing himself to be cheated. But sometime that spring the wish to get away—to flee abroad and seize the good life as had his San Jose cousin—had deepened into sickness. So he was blowing his life's savings on this malady. So what?

The man made many more trips. And on each trip, as Mr. Venkatesan sat the man down on the best rattan chair on the balcony, through the half-open door that led into the hallway he saw the women in his family gather in jittery knots. They knew he was about to forsake them.

Every brave beginning, in these cramped little islands, masked a secret betrayal. To himself, Mr. Venkatesan would always be a sinner.

Mr. Venkatesan threw himself into the planning. He didn't trust the man with the cauliflower ears. Routes, circuitous enough to fool border guards, had to be figured out. He could fly to Frankfurt via Malta, for instance, then hole up in a ship's cargo hold for the long, bouncy passage on Canadian seas. Or he could take the more predictable (and therefore, cheaper but with more surveillance) detours through the Gulf Emirates.

The go-between or travel agent took his time. Fake travel documents and work permits had to be printed up. Costs, commissions, bribes had to be calculated. On each visit, the man helped himself to a double peg of Mr. Venkatesan's whiskey.

In early September, three weeks after Mr. Venkatesan had paid in full for a roundabout one-way ticket to Hamburg and for a passport impressive with fake visas, the travel agent stowed him in the damp, smelly bottom of a fisherman's dinghy and had him ferried across the Palk Strait to Tuticorin in the palm-green tip of mainland India.

Tuticorin was the town Mr. Venkatesan's ancestors had left to find their fortunes in Ceylon's tea-covered northern hills. The irony struck him with such force that he rocked and tipped the dinghy, and had to be fished out of the sea.

The Friends of the Tigers were waiting in a palm grove for him. He saw their flashlights and smelled their coffee. They gave him a dry change of clothes, and though both the shirt and the jacket were frayed, they were stylishly cut. His reputation as an intellectual and killer (he hoped it wasn't true) of a Buddhist policeman had preceded him. He let them talk; it was not Venkatesan the schoolmaster they were praising, but some mad invention. Where he was silent from confusion and fatigue, they read cunning and intensity. He was happy to put himself in their hands; he thought of them as fate's helpers, dispatched to see him through his malady. That night one of them made up a sleeping mat for him in the the back room of his shuttered grocery store. After that they passed him from back room to back room. He spent pleasant afternoons with them drinking sweet, frothy coffee and listening to them plan to derail trains or blow up bus depots. They read his frown as skepticism and redoubled their vehemence. He himself had no interest in destruction, but he listened to them politely.

When it was safe to move on, the Friends wrote out useful addresses in Frankfurt, London, Toronto, Miami. "Stay out of refugee centers," they advised. But an old man with broken dentures who had been deported out of Hamburg the year before filled him in on which refugee centers in which cities had the cleanest beds, just in case he was caught by the wily German police. "I shan't forget any of you," Mr. Venkatesan said as two Friends saw him off at the train station. The train took him to Madras; in Madras he changed trains for Delhi where he boarded an Aeroflot flight for Tashkent. From Tashkent he flew to Moscow. He would like to have told the story of his life to his two seat mates—already the break from family and from St. Joe's seemed the stuff of adventure novels—but they were two huge and grim Uzbeks with bushels of apricots and pears wedged on the floor, under the seat, and on their laps. The cabin was noisier than the Jaffna local bus with squawking chickens and drunken farmers. He communed instead with Arnold and Keats. In Moscow the airport officials didn't bother to look too closely at his visa stamps, and he made it to Berlin feeling cocky.

At Schönefeld Airport, three rough-looking Tamil men he'd not have given the time of day to back home in Trinco grappled his bags away from him as soon as he'd cleared customs. "This is only a piss stop for you, you lucky bastard," one of them said. "You get to go on to real places while hard-working fuckers like us get stuck in this hellhole."

He had never heard such language. Up until a week ago, he would have denied the Tamil language even possessed such words. The man's coarseness shocked Mr. Venkatesan, but this was not the moment to walk away from accomplices.

The expatriate Tamils took him, by bus, to a tenement building—he saw only Asians and Africans in the lobby—and locked him from the outside in a one-room flat on the top floor. An Algerian they did business with, they said, would truck him over the border into Hamburg. He was not to look out the window. He was not to open the door, not even if someone yelled, "Fire!" They'd be back at night, and they'd bring him beer and rolls.

Mr. Venkatesan made a slow show of getting money out of his trouser pocket—he didn't have any East German money, only rupees and the Canadian dollars he'd bought on the black market from the travel agent in Trinco—but the Tamils stopped him. "Our treat," they said. "You can return the hospitality when *we* make it to Canada."

Late in the evening the three men, stumbling drunk and jolly, let themselves back into the room that smelled of stale, male smells. The Algerian had come through. They were celebrating. They had forgotten the bread but remembered the beer.

That night, which was his only night in East Germany, Mr. Venkatesan got giggly drunk. And so it was that he entered the free world with a hangover. In a narrow, green mountain pass, trying not to throw up, he said goodbye to his Algerian chauffeur and how-do-you-do to a Ghanaian-born Berliner who didn't cut the engine of his BMW during the furtive transfer.

He was in Europe. Finally. The hangover made him sentimental. Back in Trinco the day must have deepened into dusk. In the skid of tires, he heard the weeping of parents, aunts, sisters. He had looked after them as long as he could. He had done for himself what he should have ten years before. Now he wanted to walk where Shelley had walked. He wanted to lie down where consumptive Keats had lain and listened to his nightingale sing of truth and beauty. He stretched out in the back seat. When Mr. Venkatesan next opened his eyes, the BMW was parked in front of a refugee center in Hamburg.

"End of trip," the black Berliner announced in jerky English. "*Auf Wiedersehen.*"

Mr. Venkatesan protested that he was not a refugee. "I am paid up in full to Canada. You are supposed to put me in touch with a ship's captain."

The black man snickered, then heaved Mr. Venkatesan's two shiny new bags out on the street. "Goodbye. *Danke.*"

Mr. Venkatesan got out of the private taxi.

"Need a cheap hotel? Need a lawyer to stay deportation orders?"

A very dark, pudgy man flashed a calling card in his face. The man looked Tamil, but not anxious like a refugee. His suit was too expensive. Even his shirt was made of some white-on-white fancy material, though his cuffs and collar were somewhat soiled.

Mr. Venkatesan felt exhilarated. Here was another of fate's angels come to minister him out of his malady.

"The name is Rammi. G. Rammi, Esquire. One-time meanest goddamn solicitor in Paramaribo, Suriname. I am putting myself at your service."

He allowed the angel to guide him into a *rijstafel* place and feed him for free.

Mr. Venkatesan ate greedily while the angel, in a voice as uplifting as harp music, instructed him on the most prudent conduct for undocumented transients. By the end of the meal, he'd agreed to pay Rammi's cousin, a widow, a flat fee for boarding him for as long as it took Rammi to locate a ship's captain whose business was ferrying furtive cargoes.

Rammi's cousin, Queenie, lived in a row house by the docks.

Rammi had the cabdriver let them off a block and a half from Queenie's. He seemed to think cabdrivers were undercover immigration cops, and he didn't want a poor young widow bringing up a kid on dole getting in trouble for her charity.

Though Queenie had been telephoned ahead from a pay phone, she was dressed in nothing more formal than a kimono when she opened her slightly warped front door and let the men in. The kimono was the color of parrots in sunlight and reminded Mr. Venkatesan of his last carefree years, creeping up on and capturing parrots with his bare hands. In that glossy green kimono, Queenie the landlady shocked him with her beauty. Her sash was missing, and she clenched the garment together at the waist with a slender, nervous fist. Her smooth gold limbs, her high-bouncing bosom, even the stockingless arch of her instep had about them so tempting a careless sensuality that it made his head swim.

"I put your friend in Room 3A," Queenie said. "3B is less crowded but I had to put the sick Turk in it." She yelled something in German which Mr. Venkatesan didn't understand, and a girl of eight or nine came teetering out of the kitchen in adult-sized high heels. She asked the girl some urgent questions. The girl said no to all of them with shakes of her braided head.

"We don't want the fellow dying on us," Rammi said. Then they said something more in a Caribbean patois that Mr. Venkatesan didn't catch. "God knows we don't want complications." He picked up the two bags and started up the stairs.

3A was a smallish attic room blue with unventilated smoke, fitted with two sets of three-tier bunks. There were no closets, no cupboards, and on the bunk that Rammi pointed out as his, no bed linen. Four young men of indistinguishable nationality—Asia and Africa were their continents—were playing cards and drinking beer.

"Okay, 'bye," Rammi said. He was off to scout ship captains. When Rammi left, despite the company, Mr. Venkatesan felt depressed, lonely. He didn't try to get to know where the men were from and where they were headed which was how he'd broken the ice in back room dormitories in Tuticorin. One man spat into a brass spittoon. What did he have in common with these transients except the waiting?

By using his bags as a stepladder, he was able to clamber up to his allotted top bunk. For a while he sat on the bed. The men angled their heads so they could still stare at him. He lay down on the mattress. The rough ticking material of the pillow chafed him. He sat up again. He took his jacket and pants off and hung them from the foot rail. He slipped his wallet, his passport, his cloth bag stuffed with foreign cash, his new watch—a farewell present from Father van der Haagen—between the pillow and the mattress. He was not about to trust his cell mates. A little after the noon hour all four men got dressed in gaudy clothes and went out in a group. Mr. Venkatesan finally closed his eyes. A parrot flew into his dream. Mr. Venkatesan thrilled to the feathery feel of its bosom. He woke up only when Queenie's little girl charged into the room and ordered him down for lunch. She didn't seem upset about his being in underwear. She leaped onto the middle bunk in the tier across the room and told him to hurry so the food wouldn't have to be rewarmed. He thought he saw the flash of a man's watch in her hand.

Queenie had made him a simple lunch of lentil soup and potato croquettes, and by the time he got down to the kitchen it was no longer warm. Still he liked the spiciness of the croquettes and the ketchup was a tasty European brand and not the watery stuff served back home.

She said she'd already eaten, but she sat down with a lager and watched him eat. With her he had no trouble talking. He told her about St. Joe's and Father van der Haagen. He told her about his family, leaving out the part about his sister running wild in the hills with hooligans, and got her to talk about her family too.

Queenie's grandfather had been born in a Sinhalese village the name of which he hadn't cared to pass on—he'd referred to it only as "hellhole"—and from which he'd run away at age seventeen to come as an indentured laborer to the Caribbean. He'd worked sugar cane fields in British Guiana until he'd lost a thumb. Then he'd moved to Suriname and worked as an office boy in a coconut oil processing plant, and wooed and won the only daughter of the proprietor, an expatriate Tamil like him who, during the War, had made a fortune off the Americans.

He tried to find out about her husband, but she'd say nothing other than that he'd been, in her words, "a romantic moron," and that he'd hated the hot sun, the flat lands, the coconut palms, the bush, her family, her family's oil factory. He'd dreamed, she said, of living like a European.

"You make me remember things I thought I'd forgotten." She flicked her lips with her tongue until they shone.

"You make me think of doing things I've never done." He gripped the edge of the kitchen table. He had trouble breathing. "Until dinnertime," he said. Then he panted back up to his prison.

But Mr. Venkatesan didn't see Queenie for dinner. She sent word through the girl that she had a guest—a legitimate guest, a tourist from Lübeck, not an illegal transient—that evening. He felt no rage at being dumped. A man without papers accepts last-minute humiliations. He called Rammi from the pay phone in the hall.

That night Mr. Venkatesan had fun. Hamburg was not at all the staid city of burghers that Father van der Haagen had evoked for him in those last restless days of waiting in the Teachers' Common Room. Hamburg was a carnival. That night, with Rammi as his initiator into fun, he smoked his first joint and said, after much prodding, *"sehr schön"* to a skinny girl with a Mohawk haircut.

The tourist from Lübeck had been given the one nice room. Queenie's daughter had shown Mr. Venkatesan the room while the man was checking in. It was on the first floor and had a double bed with a *duvet* so thick you wanted to sink into it. The windows were covered with *two* sets of curtains. The room even had its own sink. He hadn't seen the man from Lübeck, only heard him on the stairs and in the hall on his way to and from the lavatory walking with an authoritative, native-born German tread. Queenie hadn't instructed him to stay out of sight. Secretiveness he'd learned from his bunk mates. They could move with great stealth. Mr. Venkatesan was beginning to feel like a character in Anne Frank's diary. The men in 3A stopped wearing shoes indoors so as not to be heard pacing by the tourist from Lübeck.

The tourist went out a lot. Sometimes a car came for him. From the Tourist Office, Mr. Venkatesan imagined. How nice it would be to tour the city, take a boat trip! Meantime he had to eat his meals upstairs. That was the sad part. Otherwise he felt he had never been so happy.

Every morning as soon as he got the chance he called Rammi, though he was no longer keen for Rammi to find a crooked captain. He called because he didn't want Rammi to catch on that he was feeling whatever it was that he was feeling for Queenie. Like Rammi, he didn't want complications. What he did was remind Rammi that he wouldn't go into the hold of a ship that dumped its cargo into the Atlantic. He told Rammi that both in Trinco and in Tuticorin he'd heard stories of drowned Tamils.

Mr. Venkatesan's roommates stopped going out for meals. They paid Queenie's girl to buy them cold meats and oranges from the corner store. The only thing they risked going out for was liquor. He gathered from fragments of conversation that they were all sailors, from Indonesia and Nigeria, who'd jumped ship in Hamburg harbor. Whenever they went out, he could count on the girl prowling the attic room. He let her prowl. It was almost like having Queenie in the room.

There was only one worry. The girl lifted things—small things—from under pillows. Sometimes she played under the beds where he and the other men stored their suitcases, and he heard lids swish open or closed. He didn't think the things she stole were worth stealing. He'd seen her take a handful of pfennigs from a jacket pocket once, and another time envelopes with brilliant stamps from places like Turkey and Oman. What she seemed to like best to pilfer were lozenges, even the medicated kind for sore throat. It was as if covetousness came upon her, out of the blue, making her pupils twitch and glow.

He didn't mind the loss to his roommates. But he worried that they'd get her in trouble by sending her to the store. He would have to stop her. He would have to scold her as a father might or should without messing things up with Queenie.

One morning Queenie showed up in 3A herself. "I have good news," she whispered. Two of the four men were still in bed. Mr. Venkatesan could tell they hated having a grown woman in their room. "Rammi should have word for you tonight. I'm meeting him to find out more." The morning light, streaming in through a cracked stained-glass panel in the window, put such a heavenly sheen on her face that Mr. Venkatesan blurted out in front of his roommates, "I love you, I love you."

Queenie laughed. "Hush," she said. "You're not there yet. You don't want to wake up our Teuton. I need the legitimate business too."

It seemed to Mr. Venkatesan like an invitation. He followed her down into the front hall in his night clothes. In Tamil movies heroes in his position would have been wearing brocade smoking jackets. It didn't matter. He had made his declaration. Now fate would have to sink the crooked captain and his boat.

Queenie fussed with a pink, plastic clip in her hair. She knotted and reknotted the wispy silk square around her throat. She tapped the longest fingernail he'd ever seen on the butterfly buckle of her belt. She was teasing him. She was promising he wouldn't really have to go. He wanted to stay, Anne Frank or not.

"Tonight should be a champagne night," she grinned. He saw the tensing of a dainty calf muscle as she straightened a stocking. "I'll see to coffee," she said.

Upstairs the man from Lübeck had hot water running in the bathroom sink. The pipes moaned. It was best to hide out in the kitchen until the man was back in his own room. Mr. Venkatesan joined Queenie's daughter at the dinette table. She had lozenges spread out on the tablecloth, like a sun spiked with long rays. She didn't look like a thief. She looked like a child he might have fathered if he'd married the bride his mother had picked for him in the days he'd still been considered a good catch. He hadn't married. Something dire had shown up in the conjunction of their horoscopes.

What if, just what if, what had seemed disastrous to the astrologer at the time had really been fate's way of reserving him for a better family with Queenie and this child in Hamburg?

"I'll sell you some," the child said. "I have English toffees too."

"Where?" He wanted to see her whole loot.

She ducked and brought out an old milk bottle from under the table. He saw the toffees in their red and blue wrapping papers. He saw a Muslim's worry beads. Some things in the bottle were shiny—he made out two rings among the keys and coins and coat buttons. There were two ID cards in the bottle. She reached for the cards. She had to have stolen one of the cards from a man in Room 3A. In the ID picture, which was amateurishly doctored, the roommate looked like a playboy sheikh, and not at all like a refugee without travel papers. He grabbed the roommate's card from her. It wouldn't hurt to have the fellow in his debt. The other card belonged to a very blond, very German man.

The child was shrewd. "I didn't steal anything," she snapped. "I don't know how the stuff got in that jar."

She tossed the blond man's ID to him to get rid of it, and he caught it as he had paper flowers, silk squares, and stunned rabbits hurled to front-row boys by magicians on fete days in his kindergarten. He had loved the magicians. They alone had given him what he'd wanted.

As in dreams, the burly blond man materialized out of thin

air and blocked the doorway. The man had on a touristy shirt and short pants, but he didn't have the slack gait of a vacationer. He had to be the man who lived in the nice upstairs room, the man who slept under the cozy *duvet*, who brushed his teeth in a clean, pink sink he didn't have to share, the man from whom transients like Mr. Venkatesan himself had to hide out. This man yelled something nasty in German to Queenie's daughter. The child cowered.

The man yelled again. Mr. Venkatesan started to back away. Minute by minute the man ballooned with rage.

"No *deutsch*," Mr. Venkatesan mumbled.

"You filthy swine," the man shouted in English. "We don't want you making filthy our Germany." He threw five passports down on the kitchen table and spat on the top one. "The girl, she stole something from each of you scums," he hooted.

Mr. Venkatesan recognized his in the heap of travel documents. The child must have stolen it. The child must have filched it from under his pillow while he'd slept. She was a child possessed with covetousness. Now, because of her sick covetousness, he would rot in jail. He yanked the girl by her braids and shook her. The girl made her body go limp, taking away all pleasure in hate and revenge. The tourist from Lübeck ignored the screaming child. He got on the pay phone, the one Mr. Venkatesan called Rammi on every morning. Mr. Venkatesan heard the word "*Polizei!*". He was almost fifty. By fifty a man ought to stop running. Maybe what seemed accidental now—Queenie's daughter's kleptomania blowing away his plans for escape—wasn't accidental. He remembered what had consoled Dr. Pillai at the time of his arrest. Fractals. Nothing was random, the math teacher used to say. Nothing, not even the curliness of a coastline and the fluffiness of a cloud.

Mr. Venkatesan thought about the swoops and darts of his fate. He had started out as a teacher and a solid citizen and ended up as a lusty criminal. He visualized fate now as a buzzard. He could hear the whir of fleshy wings. It hopped off a burning car in the middle of a Trinco intersection.

Then, suddenly, Queenie the beauteous, the deliverer of radiant dreams, burst through the door of the kitchen. "Leave him alone!" she yelled to the man from Lübeck. "You're harrassing my fiancé! He's a future German citizen. He will become my husband!"

THE
MANAGEMENT
OF
GRIEF

A WOMAN I don't know is boiling tea the Indian way in my kitchen. There are a lot of women I don't know in my kitchen, whispering, and moving tactfully. They open doors, rummage through the pantry, and try not to ask me where things are kept. They remind me of when my sons were small, on Mother's Day or when Vikram and I were tired, and they would make big, sloppy omelets. I would lie in bed pretending I didn't hear them.

Dr. Sharma, the treasurer of the Indo-Canada Society, pulls me into the hallway. He wants to know if I am worried about money. His wife, who has just come up from the basement with a tray of empty cups and glasses, scolds him. "Don't bother Mrs. Bhave with mundane details." She looks so monstrously pregnant her baby must be days overdue. I tell her she shouldn't be carrying heavy things. "Shaila," she says, smiling, "this is the fifth." Then she grabs a teenager by his shirttails. He slips his Walkman off his head. He has to be one of her four children, they have the same domed and dented foreheads. "What's the official word now?" she demands. The boy slips the headphones back on. "They're acting evasive, Ma. They're saying it could be an accident or a terrorist bomb."

All morning, the boys have been muttering, Sikh Bomb,

Sikh Bomb. The men, not using the word, bow their heads in agreement. Mrs. Sharma touches her forehead at such a word. At least they've stopped talking about space debris and Russian lasers.

Two radios are going in the dining room. They are tuned to different stations. Someone must have brought the radios down from my boys' bedrooms. I haven't gone into their rooms since Kusum came running across the front lawn in her bathrobe. She looked so funny, I was laughing when I opened the door.

The big TV in the den is being whizzed through American networks and cable channels.

"Damn!" some man swears bitterly. "How can these preachers carry on like nothing's happened?" I want to tell him we're not that important. You look at the audience, and at the preacher in his blue robe with his beautiful white hair, the potted palm trees under a blue sky, and you know they care about nothing.

The phone rings and rings. Dr. Sharma's taken charge. "We're with her," he keeps saying. "Yes, yes, the doctor has given calming pills. Yes, yes, pills are having necessary effect." I wonder if pills alone explain this calm. Not peace, just a deadening quiet. I was always controlled, but never repressed. Sound can reach me, but my body is tensed, ready to scream. I hear their voices all around me. I hear my boys and Vikram cry, "Mommy, Shaila!" and their screams insulate me, like headphones.

The woman boiling water tells her story again and again. "I got the news first. My cousin called from Halifax before six A.M., can you imagine? He'd gotten up for prayers and his son was studying for medical exams and he heard on a rock channel that something had happened to a plane. They said first it had disappeared from the radar, like a giant eraser just reached out. His father called me, so I said to him, what do you mean, 'something bad'? You mean a hijacking? And he said, *behn*, there is no confirmation of anything yet, but check with your neighbors because a lot of them must be on that plane. So I called poor Kusum straightaway. I knew Kusum's husband and daughter were booked to go yesterday."

Kusum lives across the street from me. She and Satish had moved in less than a month ago. They said they needed a bigger place. All these people, the Sharmas and friends from the Indo-Canada Society had been there for the housewarming. Satish and Kusum made homemade tandoori on their big gas grill and even the white neighbors piled their plates high with that luridly red, charred, juicy chicken. Their younger daughter had danced, and even our boys had broken away from the Stanley Cup telecast to put in a reluctant appearance. Everyone took pictures for their albums and for the community newspapers—another of our families had made it big in Toronto—and now I wonder how many of those happy faces are gone. "Why does God give us so much if all along He intends to take it away?" Kusum asks me.

I nod. We sit on carpeted stairs, holding hands like children. "I never once told him that I loved him," I say. I was too much the well brought up woman. I was so well brought up I never felt comfortable calling my husband by his first name.

"It's all right," Kusum says. "He knew. My husband knew. They felt it. Modern young girls have to say it because what they feel is fake."

Kusum's daughter, Pam, runs in with an overnight case. Pam's in her McDonald's uniform. "Mummy! You have to get dressed!" Panic makes her cranky. "A reporter's on his way here."

"Why?"

"You want to talk to him in your bathrobe?" She starts to brush her mother's long hair. She's the daughter who's always in trouble. She dates Canadian boys and hangs out in the mall, shopping for tight sweaters. The younger one, the goody-goody one according to Pam, the one with a voice so sweet that when she sang *bhajans* for Ethiopian relief even a frugal man like my husband wrote out a hundred dollar check, *she* was on that plane. *She* was going to spend July and August with grandparents because Pam wouldn't go. Pam said she'd rather waitress at McDonald's. "If it's a choice between Bombay and Wonderland, I'm picking Wonderland," she'd said.

"Leave me alone," Kusum yells. "You know what I want to do? If I didn't have to look after you now, I'd hang myself."

Pam's young face goes blotchy with pain. "Thanks," she says, "don't let me stop you."

"Hush," pregnant Mrs. Sharma scolds Pam. "Leave your mother alone. Mr. Sharma will tackle the reporters and fill out the forms. He'll say what has to be said."

Pam stands her ground. "You think I don't know what Mummy's thinking? *Why her*? that's what. That's sick! Mummy wishes my little sister were alive and I were dead."

Kusum's hand in mine is trembly hot. We continue to sit on the stairs.

She calls before she arrives, wondering if there's anything I need. Her name is Judith Templeton and she's an appointee of the provincial government. "Multiculturalism?" I ask, and she says, "partially," but that her mandate is bigger. "I've been told you knew many of the people on the flight," she says. "Perhaps if you'd agree to help us reach the others . . .?"

She gives me time at least to put on tea water and pick up the mess in the front room. I have a few *samosas* from Kusum's housewarming that I could fry up, but then I think, why prolong this visit?

Judith Templeton is much younger than she sounded. She wears a blue suit with a white blouse and a polka dot tie. Her blond hair is cut short, her only jewelry is pearl drop earrings. Her briefcase is new and expensive looking, a gleaming cordovan leather. She sits with it across her lap. When she looks out the front windows onto the street, her contact lenses seem to float in front of her light blue eyes.

"What sort of help do you want from me?" I ask. She has refused the tea, out of politeness, but I insist, along with some slightly stale biscuits.

"I have no experience," she admits. "That is, I have an MSW and I've worked in liaison with accident victims, but I mean I have no experience with a tragedy of this scale—"

"Who could?" I ask.

"—and with the complications of culture, language, and customs. Someone mentioned that Mrs. Bhave is a pillar—because you've taken it more calmly."

At this, perhaps, I frown, for she reaches forward, almost to take my hand. "I hope you understand my meaning, Mrs. Bhave. There are hundreds of people in Metro directly affected, like you, and some of them speak no English. There are some widows who've never handled money or gone on a bus, and there are old parents who still haven't eaten or gone outside their bedrooms. Some houses and apartments have been looted. Some wives are still hysterical. Some husbands are in shock and profound depression. We want to help, but our hands are tied in so many ways. We have to distribute money to some people, and there are legal documents—these things can be done. We have interpreters, but we don't always have the human touch, or maybe the right human touch. We don't want to make mistakes, Mrs. Bhave, and that's why we'd like to ask you to help us."

"More mistakes, you mean," I say.

"Police matters are not in my hands," she answers.

"Nothing I can do will make any difference," I say. "We must all grieve in our own way."

"But you are coping very well. All the people said, Mrs. Bhave is the strongest person of all. Perhaps if the others could see you, talk with you, it would help them."

"By the standards of the people you call hysterical, I am behaving very oddly and very badly, Miss Templeton." I want to say to her, *I wish I could scream, starve, walk into Lake Ontario, jump from a bridge*. "They would not see me as a model. I do not see myself as a model."

I am a freak. No one who has ever known me would think of me reacting this way. This terrible calm will not go away.

She asks me if she may call again, after I get back from a long trip that we all must make. "Of course," I say. "Feel free to call, anytime."

Four days later, I find Kusum squatting on a rock overlooking a bay in Ireland. It isn't a big rock, but it juts sharply out over water. This is as close as we'll ever get to them. June breezes balloon out her sari and unpin her knee-length hair. She has the bewildered look of a sea creature whom the tides have stranded.

It's been one hundred hours since Kusum came stumbling and screaming across my lawn. Waiting around the hospital, we've heard many stories. The police, the diplomats, they tell us things thinking that we're strong, that knowledge is helpful to the grieving, and maybe it is. Some, I know, prefer ignorance, or their own versions. The plane broke into two, they say. Unconsciousness was instantaneous. No one suffered. My boys must have just finished their breakfasts. They loved eating on planes, they loved the smallness of plates, knives, and forks. Last year they saved the airline salt and pepper shakers. Half an hour more and they would have made it to Heathrow.

Kusum says that we can't escape our fate. She says that all those people—our husbands, my boys, her girl with the nightingale voice, all those Hindus, Christians, Sikhs, Muslims, Parsis, and atheists on that plane—were fated to die together off this beautiful bay. She learned this from a swami in Toronto.

I have my Valium.

Six of us "relatives"—two widows and four widowers—choose to spend the day today by the waters instead of sitting in a hospital room and scanning photographs of the dead. That's what they call us now: relatives. I've looked through twenty-seven photos in two days. They're very kind to us, the Irish are very understanding. Sometimes understanding means freeing a tourist bus for this trip to the bay, so we can pretend to spy our loved ones through the glassiness of waves or in sun-speckled cloud shapes.

I could die here, too, and be content.

"What is that, out there?" She's standing and flapping her hands and for a moment I see a head shape bobbing in the waves. She's standing in the water, I, on the boulder. The tide is low, and a round, black, head-sized rock has just risen from the waves. She returns, her sari end dripping and ruined and her face is a twisted remnant of hope, the way mine was a hundred hours ago, still laughing but inwardly knowing that nothing but the ultimate tragedy could bring two women together at six o'clock on a Sunday morning. I watch her face sag into blankness.

"That water felt warm, Shaila," she says at length.

"You can't," I say. "We have to wait for our turn to come."

I haven't eaten in four days, haven't brushed my teeth.

"I know," she says. "I tell myself I have no right to grieve. They are in a better place than we are. My swami says I should be thrilled for them. My swami says depression is a sign of our selfishness."

Maybe I'm selfish. Selfishly I break away from Kusum and run, sandals slapping against stones, to the water's edge. What if my boys aren't lying pinned under the debris? What if they aren't stuck a mile below that innocent blue chop? What if, given the strong currents. . . .

Now I've ruined my sari, one of my best. Kusum has joined me, knee-deep in water that feels to me like a swimming pool. I could settle in the water, and my husband would take my hand and the boys would slap water in my face just to see me scream.

"Do you remember what good swimmers my boys were, Kusum?"

"I saw the medals," she says.

One of the widowers, Dr. Ranganathan from Montreal, walks out to us, carrying his shoes in one hand. He's an electrical engineer. Someone at the hotel mentioned his work is famous around the world, something about the place where physics and electricity come together. He has lost a huge family, something indescribable. "With some luck," Dr. Ranganathan suggests to me, "a good swimmer could make it safely to some island. It is quite possible that there may be many, many microscopic islets scattered around."

"You're not just saying that?" I tell Dr. Ranganathan about Vinod, my elder son. Last year he took diving as well.

"It's a parent's duty to hope," he says. "It is foolish to rule out possibilities that have not been tested. I myself have not surrendered hope."

Kusum is sobbing once again. "Dear lady," he says, laying his free hand on her arm, and she calms down.

"Vinod is how old?" he asks me. He's very careful, as we all are. *Is*, not was.

"Fourteen. Yesterday he was fourteen. His father and uncle were going to take him down to the Taj and give him a big birthday party. I couldn't go with them because I couldn't get two weeks off from my stupid job in June." I process bills for a travel agent. June is a big travel month.

Dr. Ranganathan whips the pockets of his suit jacket inside out. Squashed roses, in darkening shades of pink, float on the water. He tore the roses off creepers in somebody's garden. He didn't ask anyone if he could pluck the roses, but now there's been an article about it in the local papers. When you see an Indian person, it says, please give him or her flowers.

"A strong youth of fourteen," he says, "can very likely pull to safety a younger one."

My sons, though four years apart, were very close. Vinod wouldn't let Mithun drown. *Electrical engineering*, I think, foolishly perhaps: this man knows important secrets of the universe, things closed to me. Relief spins me lightheaded. No wonder my boys' photographs haven't turned up in the gallery of photos of the recovered dead. "Such pretty roses," I say.

"My wife loved pink roses. Every Friday I had to bring a bunch home. I used to say, why? After twenty odd years of marriage you're still needing proof positive of my love?" He has identified his wife and three of his children. Then others from Montreal, the lucky ones, intact families with no survivors. He chuckles as he wades back to shore. Then he swings around to ask me a question. "Mrs. Bhave, you are wanting to throw in some roses for your loved ones? I have two big ones left."

But I have other things to float: Vinod's pocket calculator; a half-painted model B-52 for my Mithun. They'd want them on their island. And for my husband? For him I let fall into the calm, glassy waters a poem I wrote in the hospital yesterday. Finally he'll know my feelings for him.

"Don't tumble, the rocks are slippery," Dr. Ranganathan cautions. He holds out a hand for me to grab.

Then it's time to get back on the bus, time to rush back to our waiting posts on hospital benches.

Kusum is one of the lucky ones. The lucky ones flew here, identified in multiplicate their loved ones, then will fly to India with the bodies for proper ceremonies. Satish is one of the few males who surfaced. The photos of faces we saw on the walls in an office at Heathrow and here in the hospital are mostly of women. Women have more body fat, a nun said to me matter-of-factly. They float better.

Today I was stopped by a young sailor on the street. He had loaded bodies, he'd gone into the water when—he checks my face for signs of strength—when the sharks were first spotted. I don't blush, and he breaks down. "It's all right," I say. "Thank you." I had heard about the sharks from Dr. Ranganathan. In his orderly mind, science brings understanding, it holds no terror. It is the shark's duty. For every deer there is a hunter, for every fish a fisherman.

The Irish are not shy; they rush to me and give me hugs and some are crying. I cannot imagine reactions like that on the streets of Toronto. Just strangers, and I am touched. Some carry flowers with them and give them to any Indian they see.

After lunch, a policeman I have gotten to know quite well catches hold of me. He says he thinks he has a match for Vinod. I explain what a good swimmer Vinod is.

"You want me with you when you look at photos?" Dr.

Ranganathan walks ahead of me into the picture gallery. In these matters, he is a scientist, and I am grateful. It is a new perspective. "They have performed miracles," he says. "We are indebted to them."

The first day or two the policemen showed us relatives only one picture at a time; now they're in a hurry, they're eager to lay out the possibles, and even the probables.

The face on the photo is of a boy much like Vinod; the same intelligent eyes, the same thick brows dipping into a V. But this boy's features, even his cheeks, are puffier, wider, mushier.

"No." My gaze is pulled by other pictures. There are five other boys who look like Vinod.

The nun assigned to console me rubs the first picture with a fingertip. "When they've been in the water for a while, love, they look a little heavier." The bones under the skin are broken, they said on the first day—try to adjust your memories. It's important.

"It's not him. I'm his mother. I'd know."

"I know this one!" Dr. Ranganathan cries out suddenly from the back of the gallery. "And this one!" I think he senses that I don't want to find my boys. "They are the Kutty brothers. They were also from Montreal." I don't mean to be crying. On the contrary, I am ecstatic. My suitcase in the hotel is packed heavy with dry clothes for my boys.

The policeman starts to cry. "I am so sorry, I am so sorry, ma'am. I really thought we had a match."

With the nun ahead of us and the policeman behind, we, the unlucky ones without our children's bodies, file out of the makeshift gallery.

From Ireland most of us go on to India. Kusum and I take the same direct flight to Bombay, so I can help her clear customs quickly. But we have to argue with a man in uniform. He has large boils on his face. The boils swell and glow with sweat as we argue with him. He wants Kusum to wait in line and he refuses to take authority because his boss is on a tea break. But

Kusum won't let her coffins out of sight, and I shan't desert her though I know that my parents, elderly and diabetic, must be waiting in a stuffy car in a scorching lot.

"You bastard!" I scream at the man with the popping boils. Other passengers press closer. "You think we're smuggling contraband in those coffins!"

One upon a time we were well brought up women; we were dutiful wives who kept our heads veiled, our voices shy and sweet.

In India, I become, once again, an only child of rich, ailing parents. Old friends of the family come to pay their respects. Some are Sikh, and inwardly, involuntarily, I cringe. My parents are progressive people; they do not blame communities for a few individuals.

In Canada it is a different story now.

"Stay longer," my mother pleads. "Canada is a cold place. Why would you want to be all by yourself?" I stay.

Three months pass. Then another.

"Vikram wouldn't have wanted you to give up things!" they protest. They call my husband by the name he was born with. In Toronto he'd changed to Vik so the men he worked with at his office would find his name as easy as Rod or Chris. "You know, the dead aren't cut off from us!"

My grandmother, the spoiled daughter of a rich *zamindar*, shaved her head with rusty razor blades when she was widowed at sixteen. My grandfather died of childhood diabetes when he was nineteen, and she saw herself as the harbinger of bad luck. My mother grew up without parents, raised indifferently by an uncle, while her true mother slept in a hut behind the main estate house and took her food with the servants. She grew up a rationalist. My parents abhor mindless mortification.

The zamindar's daughter kept stubborn faith in Vedic rituals; my parents rebelled. I am trapped between two modes of knowledge. At thirty-six, I am too old to start over and too young to give up. Like my husband's spirit, I flutter between worlds.

* * *

Courting aphasia, we travel. We travel with our phalanx of servants and poor relatives. To hill stations and to beach resorts. We play contract bridge in dusty gymkhana clubs. We ride stubby ponies up crumbly mountain trails. At tea dances, we let ourselves be twirled twice round the ballroom. We hit the holy spots we hadn't made time for before. In Varanasi, Kalighat, Rishikesh, Hardwar, astrologers and palmists seek me out and for a fee offer me cosmic consolations.

Already the widowers among us are being shown new bride candidates. They cannot resist the call of custom, the authority of their parents and older brothers. They must marry; it is the duty of a man to look after a wife. The new wives will be young widows with children, destitute but of good family. They will make loving wives, but the men will shun them. I've had calls from the men over crackling Indian telephone lines. "Save me," they say, these substantial, educated, successful men of forty. "My parents are arranging a marriage for me." In a month they will have buried one family and returned to Canada with a new bride and partial family.

I am comparatively lucky. No one here thinks of arranging a husband for an unlucky widow.

Then, on the third day of the sixth month into this odyssey, in an abandoned temple in a tiny Himalayan village, as I make my offering of flowers and sweetmeats to the god of a tribe of animists, my husband descends to me. He is squatting next to a scrawny *sadhu* in moth-eaten robes. Vikram wears the vanilla suit he wore the last time I hugged him. The *sadhu* tosses petals on a butter-fed flame, reciting Sanskrit mantras and sweeps his face of flies. My husband takes my hands in his.

You're beautiful, he starts. Then, *What are you doing here?*

Shall I stay? I ask. He only smiles, but already the image is fading. *You must finish alone what we started together*. No seaweed wreathes his mouth. He speaks too fast just as he used to when we were an envied family in our pink split-level. He is gone.

In the windowless altar room, smoky with joss sticks and

clarified butter lamps, a sweaty hand gropes for my blouse. I do not shriek. The *sadhu* arranges his robe. The lamps hiss and sputter out.

When we come out of the temple, my mother says, "Did you feel something weird in there?"

My mother has no patience with ghosts, prophetic dreams, holy men, and cults.

"No," I lie. "Nothing."

But she knows that she's lost me. She knows that in days I shall be leaving.

Kusum's put her house up for sale. She wants to live in an ashram in Hardwar. Moving to Hardwar was her swami's idea. Her swami runs two ashrams, the one in Hardwar and another here in Toronto.

"Don't run away," I tell her.

"I'm not running away," she says. "I'm pursuing inner peace. You think you or that Ranganathan fellow are better off?"

Pam's left for California. She wants to do some modelling, she says. She says when she comes into her share of the insurance money she'll open a yoga-cum-aerobics studio in Hollywood. She sends me postcards so naughty I daren't leave them on the coffee table. Her mother has withdrawn from her and the world.

The rest of us don't lose touch, that's the point. Talk is all we have, says Dr. Ranganathan, who has also resisted his relatives and returned to Montreal and to his job, alone. He says, whom better to talk with than other relatives? We've been melted down and recast as a new tribe.

He calls me twice a week from Montreal. Every Wednesday night and every Saturday afternoon. He is changing jobs, going to Ottawa. But Ottawa is over a hundred miles away, and he is forced to drive two hundred and twenty miles a day. He can't bring himself to sell his house. The house is a temple, he says; the king-sized bed in the master bedroom is a shrine. He sleeps on a folding cot. A devotee.

* * *

There are still some hysterical relatives. Judith Templeton's list of those needing help and those who've "accepted" is in nearly perfect balance. Acceptance means you speak of your family in the past tense and you make active plans for moving ahead with your life. There are courses at Seneca and Ryerson we could be taking. Her gleaming leather briefcase is full of college catalogues and lists of cultural societies that need our help. She has done impressive work, I tell her.

"In the textbooks on grief management," she replies—I am her confidante, I realize, one of the few whose grief has not sprung bizarre obsessions—"there are stages to pass through: rejection, depression, acceptance, reconstruction." She has compiled a chart and finds that six months after the tragedy, none of us still reject reality, but only a handful are reconstructing. "Depressed Acceptance" is the plateau we've reached. Remarriage is a major step in reconstruction (though she's a little surprised, even shocked, over *how* quickly some of the men have taken on new families). Selling one's house and changing jobs and cities is healthy.

How do I tell Judith Templeton that my family surrounds me, and that like creatures in epics, they've changed shapes? She sees me as calm and accepting but worries that I have no job, no career. My closest friends are worse off than I. I cannot tell her my days, even my nights, are thrilling.

She asks me to help with families she can't reach at all. An elderly couple in Agincourt whose sons were killed just weeks after they had brought their parents over from a village in Punjab. From their names, I know they are Sikh. Judith Templeton and a translator have visited them twice with offers of money for air fare to Ireland, with bank forms, power-of-attorney forms, but they have refused to sign, or to leave their tiny apartment. Their sons' money is frozen in the bank. Their sons' investment apartments have been trashed by tenants, the furnishings sold off. The parents fear that anything they sign or any money they receive will end the company's or the country's obligations to them. They fear they are selling their sons for two airline tickets to a place they've never seen.

The high-rise apartment is a tower of Indians and West Indians, with a sprinkling of Orientals. The nearest bus stop kiosk is lined with women in saris. Boys practice cricket in the parking lot. Inside the building, even I wince a bit from the ferocity of onion fumes, the distinctive and immediate Indianness of frying *ghee*, but Judith Templeton maintains a steady flow of information. These poor old people are in imminent danger of losing their place and all their services.

I say to her, "They are Sikh. They will not open up to a Hindu woman." And what I want to add is, as much as I try not to, I stiffen now at the sight of beards and turbans. I remember a time when we all trusted each other in this new country, it was only the new country we worried about.

The two rooms are dark and stuffy. The lights are off, and an oil lamp sputters on the coffee table. The bent old lady has let us in, and her husband is wrapping a white turban over his oiled, hip-length hair. She immediately goes to the kitchen, and I hear the most familiar sound of an Indian home, tap water hitting and filling a teapot.

They have not paid their utility bills, out of fear and the inability to write a check. The telephone is gone; electricity and gas and water are soon to follow. They have told Judith their sons will provide. They are good boys, and they have always earned and looked after their parents.

We converse a bit in Hindi. They do not ask about the crash and I wonder if I should bring it up. If they think I am here merely as a translator, then they may feel insulted. There are thousands of Punjabi-speakers, Sikhs, in Toronto to do a better job. And so I say to the old lady, "I too have lost my sons, and my husband, in the crash."

Her eyes immediately fill with tears. The man mutters a few

193

words which sound like a blessing. "God provides and God takes away," he says.

I want to say, but only men destroy and give back nothing. "My boys and my husband are not coming back," I say. "We have to understand that."

Now the old woman responds. "But who is to say? Man alone does not decide these things." To this her husband adds his agreement.

Judith asks about the bank papers, the release forms. With a stroke of the pen, they will have a provincial trustee to pay their bills, invest their money, send them a monthly pension.

"Do you know this woman?" I ask them.

The man raises his hand from the table, turns it over and seems to regard each finger separately before he answers. "This young lady is always coming here, we make tea for her and she leaves papers for us to sign." His eyes scan a pile of papers in the corner of the room. "Soon we will be out of tea, then will she go away?"

The old lady adds, "I have asked my neighbors and no one else gets *angrezi* visitors. What have we done?"

"It's her job," I try to explain. "The government is worried. Soon you will have no place to stay, no lights, no gas, no water."

"Government will get its money. Tell her not to worry, we are honorable people."

I try to explain the government wishes to give money, not take. He raises his hand. "Let them take," he says. "We are accustomed to that. That is no problem."

"We are strong people," says the wife. "Tell her that."

"Who needs all this machinery?" demands the husband. "It is unhealthy, the bright lights, the cold air on a hot day, the cold food, the four gas rings. God will provide, not government."

"When our boys return," the mother says. Her husband sucks his teeth. "Enough talk," he says.

Judith breaks in. "Have you convinced them?" The snaps on her cordovan briefcase go off like firecrackers in that quiet apartment. She lays the sheaf of legal papers on the coffee table. "If they can't write their names, an X will do—I've told them that."

Now the old lady has shuffled to the kitchen and soon emerges with a pot of tea and two cups. "I think my bladder will go first on a job like this," Judith says to me, smiling. "If only there was some way of reaching them. Please thank her for the tea. Tell her she's very kind."

I nod in Judith's direction and tell them in Hindi, "She thanks you for the tea. She thinks you are being very hospitable but she doesn't have the slightest idea what it means."

I want to say, humor her. I want to say, my boys and my husband are with me too, more than ever. I look in the old man's eyes and I can read his stubborn, peasant's message: *I have protected this woman as best I can. She is the only person I have left. Give to me or take from me what you will, but I will not sign for it. I will not pretend that I accept.*

In the car, Judith says, "You see what I'm up against? I'm sure they're lovely people, but their stubbornness and ignorance are driving me crazy. They think signing a paper is signing their sons' death warrants, don't they?"

I am looking out the window. I want to say, *In our culture, it is a parent's duty to hope.*

"Now Shaila, this next woman is a real mess. She cries day and night, and she refuses all medical help. We may have to—"

"—Let me out at the subway," I say.

"I beg your pardon?" I can feel those blue eyes staring at me.

It would not be like her to disobey. She merely disapproves, and slows at a corner to let me out. Her voice is plaintive. "Is there anything I said? Anything I did?"

I could answer her suddenly in a dozen ways, but I choose not to. "Shaila? Let's talk about it," I hear, then slam the door.

A wife and mother begins her new life in a new country, and that life is cut short. Yet her husband tells her: Complete what we have started. We, who stayed out of politics and came halfway around the world to avoid religious and political feuding have been the first in the New World to die from it. I no longer know what we started, nor how to complete it. I write letters to the editors of local papers and to members of Parliament. Now at least they admit it was a bomb. One MP answers back, with sympathy, but with a challenge. You want to make a difference? Work on a campaign. Work on mine. Politicize the Indian voter.

My husband's old lawyer helps me set up a trust. Vikram was a saver and a careful investor. He had saved the boys' boarding school and college fees. I sell the pink house at four times what we paid for it and take a small apartment downtown. I am looking for a charity to support.

We are deep in the Toronto winter, gray skies, icy pavements. I stay indoors, watching television. I have tried to assess my situation, how best to live my life, to complete what we began so many years ago. Kusum has written me from Hardwar that her life is now serene. She has seen Satish and has heard her daughter sing again. Kusum was on a pilgrimage, passing through a village when she heard a young girl's voice, singing one of her daughter's favorite *bhajans*. She followed the music through the squalor of a Himalayan village, to a hut where a young girl, an exact replica of her daughter, was fanning coals under the kitchen fire. When she appeared, the girl cried out, "Ma!" and ran away. What did I think of that?

I think I can only envy her.

Pam didn't make it to California, but writes me from Vancouver. She works in a department store, giving make-up hints to Indian and Oriental girls. Dr. Ranganathan has given up his commute, given up his house and job, and accepted an academic position in Texas where no one knows his story and he has vowed not to tell it. He calls me now once a week.

I wait, I listen, and I pray, but Vikram has not returned to me. The voices and the shapes and the nights filled with visions ended abruptly several weeks ago.

I take it as a sign.

One rare, beautiful, sunny day last week, returning from a

small errand on Yonge Street, I was walking through the park from the subway to my apartment. I live equidistant from the Ontario Houses of Parliament and the university of Toronto. The day was not cold, but something in the bare trees caught my attention. I looked up from the gravel, into the branches and the clear blue sky beyond. I thought I heard the rustling of larger forms, and I waited a moment for voices. Nothing.

"What?" I asked.

Then as I stood in the path looking north to Queen's Park and west to the university, I heard the voices of my family one last time. *Your time has come*, they said. *Go, be brave*.

I do not know where this voyage I have begun will end. I do not know which direction I will take. I dropped the package on a park bench and started walking.

MORE ABOUT PENGUINS

For further information about books available from Penguins in India write to Penguin Books (India) Ltd, B4/246, Safdarjung Enclave, New Delhi 110 029.

In the UK: For a complete list of books available from Penguins in the United Kingdom write to Dept. EP, Penguin Books Ltd, Harmondsworth, Middlesex UB7 0DA.

In the U.S.A.: For a complete list of books available from Penguins in the United States write to Dept. DG, Penguin Books, 299 Murray Hill Parkway, East Rutherford, New Jersey 07073.

In Canada: For a complete list of books available from Penguins in Canada write to Penguin Books Canada Ltd, 2801 John Street, Markham, Ontario L3R 1B4.

In Australia: For a complete list of books available from Penguins in Australia write to the Marketing Department, Penguin Books Australia Ltd, P.O. Box 257, Ringwood, Victoria 3134.

In New Zealand: For a complete list of books available from Penguins in New Zealand write to the Marketing Department, Penguin Books (N.Z.) Ltd, Private Bag, Takapuna, Auckland 9.

JASMINE
Bharati Mukherjee

When Jasmine Vidh, a young woman in a small Indian town, is widowed by a terrorist bomb, her fate is a life of isolation and despair. But six years later, Jasmine has become Jane Ripplemeyer, resident of Iowa and member of an unsteady and unconventional American family—a family that includes an Iowa banker, an adopted Vietnamese refugee and her own pregnant self. In following this transformation of a young life, Bharati Mukherjee has written a novel of stunning intensity, striking irony and gentle humour.

Jasmine's path through her new homeland weaves through a shifting American landscape: from Florida and the primitive brutality of the scarred Vietnam vet who brings her there; to an India recreated with stifling insularity in Queens; to Manhattan's upper west side and the exotic mystery of the self-assured young couple for whom she works. But it is in Iowa, when Bud Ripplemeyer is crippled by a desperate farmer, that Jasmine learns how completely her fate has become part of America's.

In Jasmine, Bharati Mukherjee has created a heroine as exotic and unexpected as the many worlds she lives in.

'Hers is a voice that must he heard'
— *The Ottawa Citizen*

THAT LONG SILENCE
Shashi Deshpande

That Long Silence is the story of Jaya, wife, mother of teenage children, and failed writer, whose familiar existence is disrupted when her husband is suspected of business malpractice. The family's future threatened, Jaya is confronted with difficult truths about her past. A skilful, haunting novel, *That Long Silence* is a vivid portrayal of a woman trying to erase a 'long silence' begun in childhood, rooted in herself and in the constraints of her adult life.

'A book that will change lives. Unforgettable.'
                              —*The Evening Post*